Perdue
OR
How The West Was Lost

PERDUE

OR
HOW THE WEST WAS LOST

A NOVEL BY
Geoffrey Ursell

Macmillan of Canada
A Division of Gage Publishing Limited
Toronto, Canada

CANADIAN CATALOGUING IN PUBLICATION DATA

Ursell, Geoffrey.
  Perdue, or, How the west was lost

ISBN 0-7715-9870-X

I. Title. II. Title: How the west was lost.

PS8591.R73P37 1984   C813'.54   C84-098192-9
PR9199.3.U77P37 1984

All the characters in this book are fictitious, and any resemblance to actual persons living or dead is entirely coincidental.

DESIGN: Brant Cowie/Artplus

Macmillan of Canada
A Division of Gage Publishing Limited

Printed and bound in Canada by
T. H. Best Printing Company

For Irene and Barry

Perdue
OR
How The West Was Lost

PART

1

CHAPTER ONE

MORE THAN two hundred years later, Perdue, standing on the very spot, would remember how the cavalcade, with his father in the lead on a stallion, finally came out of the forest and reached the top of the last ridge of hills. The sun was just rising behind their backs, and, from the summit of the ridge, all their shadows stretched enormously long and dark across the pale and burnished land. That vast expanse of plain seemed to pull their shadows out and out, unrolling them in wavering lines to the purple blur of the horizon.

Perdue would not remember the words his father said, words that would be paid for when his father engaged too publicly in an act that he had often enough performed in private. But Perdue would remember the pungent whirlwind of scent, the marvellous smell of wild, unbroken prairie.

Perdue would remember that smell, even though, when it first washed over him, submerging him in its fragrance, he slept. Suspended between four crossed poles, like the X dominating the centre of a game of X's and O's, his body was cradled in a hammock. Four horsemen, riding before and behind, to the right and to the left, the long poplar poles binding their horses together, carried Perdue into the unknown land.

The horsemen wore the uniforms of Hussars—long, lustrous black boots to the knees, tight scarlet riding breeches, purple- and black-velvet jackets trimmed with gold braid, silver helmets embossed with raging lions and griffins and trailing thick, feathery, pure-white plumes. Their blood-red capes hung limp in the still morning.

Although he did not see it, Perdue would remember this scene because he would hear about it many times. And although he did not consciously smell the prairie, when the scent of it later surged into his nostrils, he would recognize exactly what it was.

But Perdue would not remember what his father said that morning, because not one of all the others present would ever repeat it to him during the rest of his long, long life. He would not even hear it from his mother—carried in the same hammock, but awake and in pain—who saw, smelled, and heard everything. No, not even from the woman who had just given him birth would Perdue ever hear those violent words.

CHAPTER TWO

PERDUE SAT, his short legs dangling over the front of the oak chair, his small hands lifted to clutch at the edge of the dining-table. He could see steam rising from the plate of food that had been placed above him, but he couldn't reach it. They had forgotten the pillow again.

Perdue examined the petit-point patterns on the Irish-linen table-cloth in front of his eyes. Old Marm had done it, in Home-Across-the-Sea. It had taken sixteen years of her life. All around the outside of the cloth, piles of petit-point dead men were strewn, some in uniforms of red, with touches of white and blue, but most in blue uniforms with fleurs-de-lis on their sleeves. The entire cloth was a record of the Napoleonic Wars, from which old Marm's husband had never returned.

Further in, above Perdue's level of sight, the cloth was

full of the clamour of battle after battle—the Nile, Marengo, Trafalgar, Moscow, Leipzig—until, at the centre, the majestic Duke of Wellington confronted the cowering Napoleon at Waterloo. The table-cloth had been Old Marm's wedding gift to her only son, Sir, and his bride, Gal Sal.

That had happened long before Perdue could remember. And during all that time, the cloth, its stitching too delicate to risk the operation, had never been washed. It was filthy with smears, smudges, spatters, and mouldy particles of food, which added another dimension of texture to the patterns of thread. It was also badly stained with blood.

From his distant right, Perdue heard his father's low rumbles as he gulped down chunks of buffalo meat from a huge, roasted hump. From his distant left, he could hear the tinkle of silver on bone china as his mother stirred the last of seventeen lumps of sugar into her cup of tea.

Perdue shivered uncontrollably. His legs, bare below short pants, had turned blue, and frost clung to the soft, golden hair on his thighs. He knew that if he were properly lifted up on pillows, across the table he would be able to see a monstrous stove, glowing cherry-red from the heat it threw off. But the thick cloth, draping its red-stained folds down both sides of the table nearly to the red-stained plank floor, cut off all those warming rays. Every few minutes, Perdue heard a *clunk!* as another log dropped through a trapdoor into the stove from the self-feeding mechanism his father had invented.

There were fifty rooms in the house. And there were forty-nine stoves, and one fireplace in the lounge. The wood to feed them had been shipped in all the way from the forests in the East. At the beginning of winter, it had formed a towering pile almost as high as the two-storey barn. Now at least half of it was gone. The Help kept the self-feeding mechanisms loaded. The fires would go out instantly, quenched by the lurking cold, unless they were fed log after log.

There was no stove or fireplace in the room where the big, curved-leg bath-tub stood. It was still full of water, now solid ice, in which was trapped Perdue's flotilla of wooden warships. The Maid had taken him out of the bath, wrapped him in a towel, and rushed him into his bedroom just before the Cold Snap hit. Otherwise, Perdue might have been frozen in, ice locking itself implacably around his chubby, pink-nippled chest.

The house had been brought in sections by Red River cart, then put together by the men remaining from Sir's old company of Hussars. These men had never used hammer and nails before. Sir had to instruct them in the drill, pointing out how the hammer was to be grasped, and how the head was used to strike the nail, driving it home. Even though Sir had refused actually to pick up a hammer in the course of the demonstration, the men had learned, after a fashion.

The house, in the shape of a giant U, had risen right where Sir had wanted it, in the exact middle of a vast plain. The plain was surrounded on three sides by hills, opening to the West, across a small creek, upon unbounded prairie. There was nothing else on the plain, not a tree, not a bush, not a plant higher than the top of Sir's gleaming black-leather cavalry boots.

A massive oak door at the front of the house opened into a lobby, then the lounge (with its fireplace), the drawing-rooms and dining-room to one side, the billiard room and Sir's library and study to the other. The south wing sheltered the kitchens and pantries, the serving rooms, store-rooms, china cupboard, wine vault, the safe, and the bedrooms of the Maid and the Help. The north wing included the family and guest bedrooms, dressing-rooms, and the room with the bath-tub.

Unfortunately, the men did not learn their building drill

as well as they should have. They managed to piece the sections together, but only at the cost of leaving large cracks between. Each room was intact, but the rooms only clutched at each other from a distance. Every time Perdue passed shivering from one room to another, he could see, between long iron spikes, a view of The Great Outdoors.

Far away in the white, white space out there, visible between the cracks on three sides of the house—north, south, and east (beyond the barn and the woodpile)—a thin line of bluer white glistened. Above that line, barely moving brown specks dotted the brooding white folds of the hills. The specks were the last of the buffalo, and the thin blue line was a barrier of bone, of buffalo bone.

CHAPTER THREE

EARLIER, IN THE FALL, after they had finished the house, Sir had furnished the men with Lee-Enfield repeating rifles and marched them out one afternoon and evening to where he imagined the northern limits of his estate should be, just at the foot of the encircling hills. Perdue went with them, perched in front of his father, on the jet-black back of the stallion, Stud. The taxidermist and his crew would follow the next morning. They passed through the midst of the uncountable numbers of buffalo that grazed the lush plain during the day, inexplicably retreating at dusk to the surrounding hills to sleep in the coulees and draws.

Around the camp-fire that night, the men danced to the frolicking whine of a fiddle, falling instantly asleep where they dropped in the grass and buffalo dung. The next morning, before the buffalo began to come down from the hills, Sir strung the men out in a ragged line. As the buffalo came plodding towards them, towards the grass behind the men, the men began to shoot.

They shot all morning, all afternoon. Perdue carried ammunition up and down the line. He watched the barrels of the rifles grow hotter and hotter, until the bullets sizzled out of them. He lived all that day with the smell of acrid gun smoke, the smell of sweating men, the sweet and ever-more-powerful odour of fresh blood. They shot and they shot, a thin line of men creating a growing mound of animal corpses.

The buffalo, desperate to reach the succulent grass, kept plodding straight ahead, climbing over the bodies before them, hooves sinking into warm flesh. They stumbled on, struggling up and over the pile. As they reached the top, the men shot them and they slumped down. The sun floated across the sky, dying in a dark-red glare. Finally, as the men were shooting almost straight up in the air, the buffalo in front of them stopped trying to reach their pasture. The buffalo from the other ranges of hills, which had been grazing placidly all day behind the backs of the men, also turned towards their bedding-places.

Sir sent several of the men to slice off some of the delicious humps and to sever the sweet tongues, and that night the men feasted.

The next day, the taxidermist and his assistants arrived before breakfast. They had left the house before sunrise. Now the assistants quickly began their work, deftly cutting the shaggy heads free of the bodies, building a large mound of heads beside the table where the taxidermist stood. Perdue watched the taxidermist clean out the heads. With steel instruments sharper than razors he sliced out the flesh of the throat and the mouth, flipped the eyes out with two flicks of his wrist, sawed an opening into the brain-pan from below, and pulled the brain clear in one swift movement. The assistants brought heads from bodies and carried cleaned heads away to dry in rows in the sun.

Over the camp-fires, sliced buffalo brain sizzled in the frying-pans. Sir and his men devoured it eagerly. Then they broke camp and left for the southern hills. Perdue rode in front of his father again, cradled by his strong arms.

Again they shot buffalo all day. Again they feasted on tongue and hump. Again the taxidermist arrived in the morning.

The third day they moved to the eastern hills. The blood of the beasts had been flowing along the lines of bodies and down towards the river, swelling the slow trickle of water to a thick, red stream. Now, to reach the river, the blood had to flow past the men. The bodies had created a dam, and the blood gathered at the foot of the mound of bodies and began to move towards the men in a thick, slow wave. Still the buffalo came, and still the men shot and shot and shot. The blood mounted higher. It reached the feet of the men, flowed beyond them, towards the distant house.

All that day the buffalo came, the men shot, the blood rose higher and higher. The men stood up to shoot. The blood rose to their knees. By afternoon the entire plain was covered with blood, a lake of blood that lapped at the foundations of the house and barn and woodpile, circled them, flowed ponderously towards the river. The blood bore with it tons of buffalo turds and thousands of drowned gophers, bull snakes, garter snakes, rattle-snakes. Hundreds of hawks wheeled through the air, plucking bodies out of the blood at their leisure. They uttered insane cries of joy.

Perdue carried ammunition, sloshing through warm fluid up to his belly. As the day wore on, he held the boxes of shells high, arms upraised above the red flow that swirled around his chest. Finally, only by lifting his chin in the air could Perdue keep his mouth free to breathe, although the hot fumes of blood filled his nose, the hot taste of blood trickled into his mouth. And only then did Sir, splashing towards him on Stud, lift him dripping up into the saddle.

Evening came, and the men waded back to the house. In rows covering the entire roof, eyeless buffalo heads stared blindly out at the prairie, awaiting new, glass eyes.

Inside, around a table that was nearly afloat in the blood, the men drank twenty kegs of whisky and gorged themselves once more on fried buffalo hump and tongue. They sang battle songs uproariously. Until, stuffed and drunk, they clambered onto the table, falling in heaps on top of the army of petit-point dead men, and slept.

Miles downstream, a tribe of Indians had camped at the favourite autumn campsite, in a wide bend of river-bottom meadow. All were asleep, except for two lovers, who lay on the rim of the river valley. In the midst of love, they felt the ground tremble. And glancing down at the moonlit camp, they saw it swallowed up in a moving wall of silvery-red that left no life behind, smelled the stench of blood and death, and thought the world was coming to an end.

That night, at the site of the buffalo slaughter, the howling of hundreds of packs of wolves and coyotes reverberated through the pale sheen of the waning moon. Then all was silent, as the scavengers ravenously gulped meat from bloating carcasses. By morning, they had eaten their way through all three sides of the dam of bodies, and what little remained of the lake of blood surged out, emptying the vast and sodden plain.

And by the light of the blood-red sunrise, the land was revealed, free of life, and ready—after the passage of the coming winter—to be farmed.

CHAPTER FOUR

PERDUE WOKE UP in darkness. He thought that he might have slipped underneath the ten layers of feather quilts, down into the sagging hollow that was the centre of his bed. But when he blew a hard breath and ice crystals fluttered back down upon his face, he knew that at least his head was free. Then he moved his arms up along his sides and touched the empty air with small, waving motions of his hands. It was dark, but he felt it should be morning.

The stove in his room had gone out, yet it wasn't really very cold. And the usual keening whistle of wind knifing through his room had ceased. Perdue decided to wait until someone came and started the fire in his room again. Then he felt the urgent pressure that had suddenly made itself known in his bladder.

Reluctantly, Perdue wriggled his way up towards the

head of the bed, fighting free of the cosy cocoon that grasped him. He slid off the bed, his naked feet sinking into the layers of buffalo fur that covered and softened all the floors. He knelt by the chamber pot. The pee, steaming, sizzled against the icy porcelain, but did not immediately turn to yellow ice, as it did on other mornings.

Quickly, Perdue dressed in the clothes Sir thought suitable for a young boy: string-net underwear, short-sleeve cotton shirt, short pants, open-weave sandals. Sir had worn exactly the same outfit when he had been as young as Perdue, back in Home-Across-the-Sea.

Out in the hall, all was still. And totally dark. There was no light coming through the windows or the cracks between the rooms. In fact, where the nearest crack had been, a door of solid snow had blown across the hall, closing it off. But through the snow door, Perdue could feel where the shape of a man had been punched.

He followed the hall to the central portion of the house, moving cautiously, feeling his way. All the stoves were out, in every room. He passed through the library, the billiard room, the lounge. Through the dining-room, the drawing-rooms, each with its door of snow with a man-shape punched through.

From far down the hall of the other wing, Perdue heard noises, as of something being smashed into a wall, saw the pale glow of a lantern. Moving as quietly as he could, Perdue reached the kitchen door. There was Sir, supervising, and the Maid, holding the lantern, as the Help swung an axe, chopping the rough opening of a door through the outside boards of the kitchen wall. A shovel leaned beside the opening.

"Blizzard," Sir announced, apparently not having noticed Perdue, but speaking to him anyway. "Have to dig our way out."

Perdue knew that all the doors of the house, having been shipped from Home-Across-the-Sea, where such things as blizzards did not have to be considered, opened outwards. As the men had been hanging them, the Help had said, "These doors are going wrong." Sir didn't know then what the Help had meant. Now he did.

"Couldn't get any wood since midnight. Lucky thing she drifted," the Help said between swings. Putting the axe down and picking up a meat cleaver, the Help began to cut blocks out of the snow.

"Here," Sir told Perdue, "pile these along the wall."

Perdue grabbed the first block of snow, staggered under its solid bulk to the nearest wall and placed it carefully in the corner.

Perdue's arms were red and raw. His whole body ached with fatigue. He had filled the spare pantries, the spare servant's bedroom, and had finally lined one entire wall of the hall with blocks of snow. First he had piled them as high as he could lift them around the edges of the rooms. Then he had stood on a chair to raise them another couple of levels. Sir had commanded the operation. It was Sir who had thought of the chair.

The tunnel the Help was carving through the snow had become as long as the hall, and then longer. Perdue had to make the trek down its dim white length, past the lanterns placed at intervals on the blood-coloured grass that the tunnel floor uncovered, to fetch each block of snow. The grass crackled and slithered against Perdue's legs, slicing innumerable tiny welts in his bare flesh.

Perdue was standing at the Help's side, waiting for yet another block, the ten thousand and forty-sixth according to Sir's count, when the shovel broke through. The stinging, frigid outside air pushed in with a *woosh!!*

"Run for it! Run!" the Help yelled, taking to his heels. "Before she freezes us stiff!"

They dashed back down the tunnel, where the Maid had buffalo coats and buffalo hats and buffalo leggings and buffalo boots and buffalo mitts waiting for them.

Sir, already dressed for The Great Outdoors, strode before them. "After me, chaps," he said. He bulled through the remaining barrier of snow. They followed.

Perdue had never known such light, such cold. Though he closed his eyes at once, the light pushed through his lids, dazzling his vision. He took tiny sips of the glacial air that stung his throat, his lungs. His breath came back out of his body laden with moisture and instantly froze into clouds of ice crystals.

Tilting his head, Perdue felt the sun through his clenched-shut eyes as a massive, blazing, fiercely white disc. He could not move because he could not see. He was blind with light. At last, by covering his eyes with his mitts and forming small peep-holes, Perdue could begin to look at the world of snow around him.

He saw the dark, furry shapes of Sir and the Help striding off around the south end of the drift to try to find the barn and the woodpile beside it. Perdue turned around and looked towards the house. Where the house should have been was only a hill of snow. Perdue began climbing.

From the very top of the hill, he could see for miles and miles in all directions. The sky overhead was a flawless blue, through which the sun burned a huge, white hole. On either side of the sun a fiery, circling ring joined two dazzling echoes of the sun, smaller suns. None of the bushes near the river were visible: all were buried deep in snow. There were no brown dots on the hillsides: the few remaining buffalo must have huddled in the deepest coulees they could find to wait out the storm.

Around the house the blizzard had shaped a mighty bow wave, which had risen up and engulfed the entire building. The barn and the woodpile, in the lee of the house, were quite free of snow. Perdue could see Sir and the Help now, gathering wood and pointing towards the house. It was true: if they had cut through the wall nearest the barn, they would have broken free much more easily.

A small stir of wind, eddying across the prairie, wrapped itself around Perdue. It brought to his nostrils the faint odour of something dead, the rank smell as of a carcass that had been melting in the blaze of the hottest summer day. Perdue turned to face the wind, but the smell was gone.

When he turned back again, he saw Sir beckon, so Perdue lay down on his back, pointed his feet in the direction of the barn, and pushed off. The slope was smooth and steep and Perdue raced down it, gathering speed. As he slid, Perdue began to spin, at first slowly, then totally out of control. Until at last he came to rest at the feet of the men, spinning, spinning, spinning like a top.

GEOFFREY URSELL

CHAPTER FIVE

IT WAS NIGHT, but Perdue could not rest. Long after everyone had gone to bed, he lay awake, waiting for a moment when he knew he would be called upon to arise. The moment came.

Perdue released himself from the clutches of his bed. He stood up. He walked to the doorway and listened. Snug within the insulation of the massive snow-drift, the house was almost soundless. Nothing from the outside world could penetrate.

It would also have been very, very dark, as a tunnel in a mine far underground is dark, except that the stoves were glowing beacons. They only needed a few of them now, and, for these, the Help had dug down through the snow to clear the chimneys. By the dull-red glow of the stoves, Perdue stole through the house. He could silently explore at least forty-seven (and sometimes forty-eight, when the

Help spent the night with the Maid) of the fifty rooms. The room of Sir and Gal Sal he never entered, not even in the day, when all the lanterns were lit.

Perdue prowled across the wall-to-wall buffalo rug. Past the bathroom where his wooden fleet had started to break free from the grip of the ice. Past the thirteen bedrooms for guests. Past the room of Sir and Gal Sal. Past the shelf upon shelf, right up to the ceiling, of leather-bound books. Past the massive table in the middle of the billiard room, settees and chairs all around, and a bar with a mirror all along one wall. Into the lounge, with its stone fireplace, the stones dragged out of the hills and shaped into an opening where an entire buffalo could be roasted on an iron spit.

Perdue stood in the centre of the lounge. Two stoves in the corners farthest from the fireplace throbbed dully in the murky air. The thick red light they shed glinted again and again from the thousands of eyes, glass eyes stuck into the sockets of mounted buffalo heads that hung tier upon tier upon tier. Three walls were covered with mounted heads. The fireplace wall was bare, awaiting, Sir had said, a suitable specimen.

Perdue looked at the glinting eyes and began to lose himself in their glassy depths. Light reflected from them, thousands of specks of light that seemed to give life to the eyes. The gaze of the buffalo eyes followed Perdue as he took a few hesitant steps.

He thought he could hear once more the living buffalo, grunting, snorting, bellowing. Then the room filled up with sounds and he was engulfed by a mighty herd that could, at a noise out of place, at a strange smell, leap into flight, into thundering stampede.

But they did not. They watched Perdue. They had him almost surrounded. He was at their mercy. They were about to ask him a question, and Perdue was afraid of what it might be. He backed away. He backed right out of the room.

Still, the noises were there. Perhaps even louder. And they grew louder and louder as Perdue moved away from the buffalo, moved closer to the room of Sir and Gal Sal. Perdue stopped at their room, put his eye to the keyhole.

The damper on the stove had been opened, throwing out wide bars of flickering red illumination. On the bed, riding an imaginary horse, was Sir. On the floor was a creature covered in the hide of a white buffalo calf. The creature grunted, snorted, bellowed, prancing around the room. Its long, curling blonde hair hung down below its budding horns and hid its face.

Sir had shot the white calf on the very spot where the house was placed. He thought it was a favourable omen for his plans.

Sir bounced on the bed, always keeping his front to the calf. The bed squeaked and groaned. As Sir rode faster and faster, his thing started to stiffen. The calf turned its behind to Sir, kicked its legs in the air. All at once, Sir's thing grew enormously, jutting out from his body. With one bound he leapt from the bed, grabbed the calf's hindquarters with his hands, and shoved his thing at its behind until it disappeared from view. Perdue was astonished.

Then both the calf and Sir were grunting, whimpering, moaning, and the voice of Gal Sal came out of the calf's mouth, "Oh shoot me! Oh shoot me! Oh shoot!" And they both convulsed, grunting and giving little screams. Then the calf collapsed to the floor and Sir, still joined to it, followed.

The red light of the room made it look as if the eye watching at the keyhole glinted, was made of glass.

CHAPTER SIX

PERDUE STOOD on the ramparts of the snow fort the Help had made for him, looking in the direction of the drifts that covered the shacks and stables the Hussars had built along the creek. From across the crusted snow came shouts of "Huzza! Huzza!" and then the Hussars, bodies enveloped in enormous buffalo coats, the breath of their horses steaming from flared nostrils, charged down upon him. Swirling past, they raced on towards the hills, their cheers fading in the still, icy air.

Perdue watched them until they disappeared, dwindling to small motes of darkness that rose to the top of the highest ridge of white, stood out momentarily against the clear blue of the sky, then dropped out of sight. He waited for them to return. Waited until he understood that they were gone.

All that week, Perdue tried to avoid being near Sir.

"Bloody raggers," Sir kept complaining. "Bloody run amuck without me! Cashier the lot! Give 'em claws for breakfast!" And he threw back another glass of whisky, neat.

At night, Perdue lay with a pillow over his head, to shut out the groans and shouts, and once the sound of a whip, which echoed down the hall to his bedroom.

From the top of the high drift that covered the house, Perdue saw a cluster of dark specks crest the ridge of hills and move towards him. After a time, he heard the jingle of harness bells ringing faintly through the air, and laughter, the trill of women's laughter. As they came closer, Perdue saw that the Hussars had returned, outriders circling an enormous sleigh. The sleigh, pulled by a dozen horses, was filled with women, all bundled up so that only their faces were showing. And behind the sleigh, skittering across the snow at the end of a thick rope, was a huge dark-green tree.

As they neared the house, the men on horses and the women in the sleigh began to sing.

Deck the halls with boughs of holly!
Fa-la-la-la-la, la-la, la, la!
'Tis the season to be jolly!
Fa-la-la-la-la, la-la, la, la!

Fast away the old year passes!
Fa-la-la, la-la-la, la, la, la!
Praise the new, ye lads and lasses!
Fa-la-la-la-la, la-la, la, la!

And they kept on singing, until, with a great shout, they all came to a halt by the tunnel that led into the house.

Perdue watched Sir rush out to greet them.

"Bloody muffs," he exclaimed. "Thought you'd shoved the moon. Gone to whip the cat! Gone to find a hossy-gossy! Bloody lot of clappers!"

He shook all the men's hands vigorously, thudded them

on the back, and kissed every woman welcome. Leaving the Help to attend to the horses, Sir led them all, with their parcels and trunks and travelling bags, into the house.

Working quickly in the freezing cold, the Hussars cleared away that part of the drift that covered the east wall of the dining-room. With metal bars, several of them pried the wall off, letting it fall flat on the snow. Others, each holding a branch, dragged the tree inside the house. At once, the wall was lifted up again, hammers drove the spikes back into place, and shovels flung the snow against the wall until it disappeared behind the mound of white.

The geese, set free from the baskets in which they had travelled, shook their wings and stretched out their necks. They began to waddle aimlessly across the snow, their distended bodies rocking on thin orange legs.

Sir raised his sabre high, held it poised for a moment, then swung it whistling down. The Hussars, Sir in the lead on Stud, charged. They screamed their battle cry, "Chumber!! Chumber!! Chumber!!"

The Hussars, with Sir giving the command, swung sabres free from sheaths. Their horses pawed the ground, snorting.

Sir raised his sabre high, held it poised for a moment, then swung it whistling down. The Hussars, Sir in the lead on Stud, charged. They screamed their battle cry, "Chumber!! Chumber!! Chumber!!"

Perdue saw the geese try to flap their wings, to lift their overstuffed bodies off the ground, to fly. They honked desperately. The sabres whirled, cold steel flashing in the frost-white air. Head after head fell upon the snow. The headless bodies still ran, gouts of blood spurting out, staining the white feathers.

The Hussars pulled up their horses, making the rear hooves carve grooves in the snow. They wheeled, horses prancing, holding their sabres, glistening with frozen blood, high.

The headless geese raced about, finally falling down, feet feebly kicking.

The white snow was traced with mysterious patterns of blood.

At his small table in the corner, garlanded like the large one with boughs of holly, Perdue watched the Hussars and their consorts finish the Christmas feast. They had eaten roast goose stuffed with truffles, roast turkey with cranberry sauce, roast beef with horse-radish. They had drunk sherry, whisky, red wine, white wine, champagne. Now, swallowing pieces of mince pie and plum pudding flamed with brandy, they sipped port. The Maid and the Help, exhausted from cooking and serving, hovered nearby, ready to pour coffee and tea.

The men had unbuttoned the top buttons of their uniforms, the women had eased the stays of their dresses. Now they leaned towards each other, whispering and laughing, touching each other on the arms, waists, thighs. Sir and Gal Sal, at opposite ends of the long table, smiled at each other lasciviously.

In the open hearth, a great fire roared high. On the other side of the room stood the tree. Its symmetrical branches, thick with dark-green needles, were festooned with coloured balls of glass. Small silver angels hung in a hovering choir everywhere upon it. Balancing in silver holders, candles burned at the tip of every branch. And on the very pinnacle of the tree, almost touching the ceiling, a bigger candle blazed, throwing gleaming light off a great star of gold. All around the room, the candle flames glinted, flickering in the thousands of buffalo eyes.

The wrapping of presents lay strewn about. Perdue looked at his present, which lay on the table in front of him: a fire kit with a flint and striking stone. He picked it up, holding the flint in one hand and the striking stone in the other. He hit them together. Showers of sparks shot off, small constellations of fire.

CHAPTER SEVEN

ONE MORNING Perdue woke up and sunlight was flooding through his window, warm breezes wafting through the cracks in his room. The snow had melted. It was spring.

By the next day, the land was dry enough to plough. In the barn the matched team of sixteen Percheron mares was restless, scenting the awakening grass. The Help led them out, harnessed them two by two into the traces attached to a giant disc harrow.

The round blades of the harrow gleamed in the sun. The Help had spent weeks in the winter honing their edges, readying them to slice into the fabric of grass, into the prairie wool that covered the rich loam below, to turn the soil over into furrows ready to receive the wheat seed.

Poised above and in front of the blades was a small metal seat. And a lever to lower the blades into the earth. The

Help climbed up and sat down, gathering all the reins in his hands. He clucked to the horses and they lurched forward, easily pulling the harrow across the field.

Sir mounted Stud, reaching down to lift Perdue up in front of him. Then they followed the harrow, Sir eager to watch the first moment when the land itself would begin to know his mastery.

They rode directly to the East. When the harrow had come within a stone's throw of the barrier of buffalo bones, Sir shouted "Here!" And the Help dropped the lever and the circling blades fell upon the earth, splitting open and turning over the cover of grass to expose the moist, dark soil.

The glossy grey coats of the Percherons shone in the light, and light reflected off the polished brass harness trim. The team, full of spirit, pulled the harrow swiftly, the blades moving like razors through soft flesh. Sir brought Stud to a halt, and sat watching as the other horses jingled into the distance, the straight furrows of exposed earth steaming in the heat.

By the time the Help did not come in for supper it was too late to go look for him. An evening storm had pounced out of the hills, bringing a torrent of rain and incredible lightning. Sir tried to send Perdue, but he could get no further than the barn before he had to take shelter. The rain came down so hard by this time that, when Perdue held a hand in front of him, it disappeared. So he had to stay in the barn all night, falling asleep on a big pile of loose hay that had tumbled out of the loft.

When Perdue woke at first light, the team of horses stood above him, the leaders cropping at the hay near his feet and head. They trembled, exhausted, bodies thick with mud. Two of the horses, in the centre of the hitch, had been struck by lightning and killed instantly. The others, terrified, could do nothing to rid themselves of the smouldering bodies except run and run and run. And still the dead beasts stayed with them, dragged along the ground, smashed with hooves, bones broken, until the corpses were almost unrecognizable.

The Help was not with them.

Nor was the harrow. The single-tree was snapped off where it had been bolted to the machine.

Perdue got up as quietly as he could and circled away from the team. They stood, heads hanging, slick with mud and froth, quivering and shuddering uncontrollably. He reached the ladder leading up to the loft, then into the lantern on top of the roof. Perdue climbed all the way up into the lantern, lifting up the trapdoor and letting it fall behind him. The eight-sided wooden wall was no higher than his chest. The wall was topped by eight wooden pillars, holding aloft a cupola, upon which perched a large weather-vane in the shape of a prancing horse.

From this vantage point, high above the house, Perdue could trace the outline of what had happened in the pattern of turned earth and mud. The Help had guided the team around and around the long, long boundaries of the farm, moving slowly away from the bone barriers and the barrier of the river in an almost-imperceptibly tightening rectangle. Perhaps a quarter-mile of prairie on all four sides had been transformed in this way.

Then the rhythm had been broken, precisely where Perdue could not determine from such a distance. The rest of the land was laced with a crazy criss-cross of ploughed furrows, patterned like the web of a demented spider. The horses had been turned, time and again, back from the barriers of bone and water, to race once more the length and breadth of the land. The lever holding the discs down had apparently locked into place, and although the blades sometimes bounced clear, they then buried themselves back in with renewed force.

At last, Perdue spotted something glinting in the sunrise that must be the harrow itself, far in the north-west corner of the land. And near it a moving speck — the Help? No. A horse, a black horse and rider.

Perdue began to unhitch the horses, working from the rear of the team to the front. He led them into their stalls, where, after gulping the bucket of water he gave to each one, they dropped down and immediately slept. By the time Perdue had nearly finished with the horses, Sir had returned.

"Never find the poor bugger," he announced. "Must have fallen off. Harrow sliced him up. Horses went over him. Pity. Have to get another one. Won't get the crop in as fast as we ought."

This was the longest speech Perdue had ever heard Sir make. He was clearly upset at the delay.

"Let's have breakfast," he said. "Need some bloody good meat in our guts."

Perdue could not stop the spew of almost-completely digested buffalo-tongue stew that burst from his mouth, slopping down the front of Sir's riding breeches and all down his high, polished, black riding boots.

CHAPTER EIGHT

THE HOUSE FLOATED on a pale-green sea. The sea dimpled and rippled in the small breeze.

From the lantern of the barn, Perdue watched through his father's field-glasses as the survey crew clambered over the barrier of bone to the North and began to walk upon the sea. They trampled a line straight as the path of a bullet, passing only a couple of metres from the front door of the house. Every so often they pushed a wooden stake into the ground. No one in the house noticed. The survey crew moved on, coming to a halt at the barrier of bone in the South, then moving off towards the shacks of the Hussars.

At dinner that night, as Sir carved thick slices from the buffalo-hump roast, they thought they heard the sound of thunder, a storm rumbling out of the North. Neither Sir nor Gal Sal paid it any more attention. Perdue, however, thought it sounded different from a storm.

The dynamite blast that cleared a wide path through the northern barrier occurred as they were finishing the meal. Fragments of bone were shot into the air and scattered in a million directions. When some of them came down upon the roof of the house, it sounded like a spring shower.

"Good for the crop," Sir pronounced.

The next morning somebody pounding furiously on the front door woke them all up. Sir went to answer, tucking his night-shirt into his breeches. Perdue staggered along behind him, rubbing the sleep out of his eyes.

"God damn it! Open up in there! Come on, you sonofa-bitch, open up!!"

Sir had picked up an elephant gun, a huge, double-barrelled .550 magnum Express, on the way to the door. It was his favourite weapon, since it could knock down an elephant in full charge. Sir shouted, "Stand clear!" Then he kicked the door open and levelled the gun.

The man in front of them wore the uniform of a train conductor. A crowd of people stood behind him, wearing baggy dark clothes, sheepskin coats, and colourful, printed kerchiefs. Behind all of them, no further than Sir could spit, dark metal and black enamel gleaming in the first rays of sun, an enormous locomotive loomed up.

"You god damn Station Masters are getting worse all the time!" the Conductor shouted. "Didn't you know we were running late?!"

Sir raised the gun to firing position.

"What the hell are you up to now?!" demanded the Conductor.

Perdue opened his mouth to speak.

The Conductor leaned over to hear what Perdue was going to say. The immigrants had already thrown themselves flat on the front veranda, which, it had to be admitted, did very closely resemble a station platform. Especially with a train on the tracks in front of it.

"What the hell?" asked the Conductor as he saw Sir's trigger finger tightening.

Not caring if the Conductor moved any further out of the way or not, Sir let go with both barrels of the Express. The top of the Conductor's splendid blue hat was instantly transformed into minute shreds of cloth. And the engine, which had been peacefully hissing steam, now smashed in the very guts of its vital workings, issued forth with a massive gush of steam and boiling water and fragments of metal that fortunately was carried out the other side of the machine by the force of the bullets in their flight.

"You can't—" the Conductor blurted.

Sir stepped forward, grabbed the handle of the door, and swung it shut. "Bloody trespassers," he said.

The young man in the red uniform stood very politely by Sir's desk, sipping tea out of one of Gal Sal's favourite Doulton china cups with the Coronation portraits on it. He tried to explain the circumstances to Sir once more.

"Bloody railway," Sir muttered. "Bloody foreigners."

"It's an unfortunate situation," the young man said. "However, the railway has been given the authority by the Government of the country to place its main line and its stations wherever it thinks best."

"Not on my bloody land," Sir replied.

"I'm afraid so, Sir."

"Bloody hills are filling up with bloody foreigners and their bloody little sod hovels. Bloody railway ships in load after bloody load. What's the bloody country coming to, eh?"

"The railway has agreed not to press charges about the engine. The Prime Minister had a word with them."

"Bloody well better have! Saved his life more than once. Bloody coward!"

The young man placed his cup on Sir's leather-topped desk. The cup began to assume a life of its own, jingling against its saucer in a barely noticeable way.

"He has instructed them about that," the young man gave assurances.

The cup jingled harder, clinking against the saucer. Indeed, the entire room was coming to strange, convulsive life before Perdue's eyes. The glass chandelier trembled and tinkled. The shelves of books jiggled. The very floor and walls and ceiling began to shudder.

"But what about the bloody tracks?!" Sir demanded. "What's the bloody coward done about the bloody tracks!?"

A low rumbling noise started to fill the room. The massive, solid-oak desk started hopping in place, thudding against the vibrating floor. The noise quickly grew louder, a continuous thundering roar that built and built. The tea service danced across the desk top, clearing papers out of its path. Books slid onto their sides, toppled from their shelves. Perdue scurried about, trying vainly to keep things in their place.

The young man had to shout, "The railway won't listen to him on that!"

Sir screamed back, over the deafening roar, "Bloody hell!! I'll blow the bastards off the track then!!"

He hoisted the elephant gun, which he kept by his side all the time now. He tried to walk to the window, but the floor kept bouncing him back to where he had started.

The chandelier was leaping on its cord, spewing glass brilliants all over the room. Whole shelves of books tumbled, thudding down. Chairs overturned. The desk was doing callisthenics, jumping on the spot.

The young man in the red uniform was screaming at the top of his lungs, "Don't, Sir!! Don't!!" He couldn't take a step from the place where he was being bounced up and down on the soles of his large boots.

Perdue clung to the side of the desk.

Sir tried to rest the gun on his shoulder. It shook violently in his hands.

Perdue barely heard the words, as Sir screamed them out, "God damn the CPR!!!"

A horrifying, ear-splitting mechanical shriek pierced the room. Perdue tried to clasp his hands over his head, couldn't keep them in place. His hands kept slapping his head harder and harder. The floor flung him up and down, up and down. The entire house, it seemed, was now leaping several feet into the air again and again. The spikes in the wood squealed and groaned. Some, loosening their hold, shot dangerously across the room, penetrating the opposite walls. Then a new and even louder sound assailed them, the terrible screech of metal sliding upon metal.

No one heard the explosion from the gun. One moment they were looking for the train through a window. The next, the glass billowed out as if in silent, slow motion, and almost at the same instant the engine completely filled their view and then the coal car and the passenger cars flashed by as the train thundered down the tracks, brakes screaming in an attempt to slow it from full speed to a dead stop by the time it reached the end of the line at the new station only a few miles down the track. The sound of the wailing whistle and the squealing brakes went from a high to a lower pitch in a moment.

Perdue thought he heard Sir yell again, "Bloody Doppler! Bloody German!" But he really couldn't be sure he was hearing anything any more.

Gradually the room stopped shaking, the noise abated.

Sir *was* speaking. The young man looked as if he were asking what Sir was saying. Perdue knew that Sir must be complaining that this happened at all hours of the day and night. Never the same hours, because the train never ran on time.

The young man was shaking his head no. He saluted Sir, turned on his heel, and left. Sir tipped a chair back up and sat down at his desk. Perdue moved near to him. He thought he could hear Sir saying something.

It was this.

"Missed! I've never bloody missed in all my life. Missed a bloody great train. I hope they never hear about it down at The Club. God damn the bloody CPR!"

CHAPTER NINE

THE WHEAT WAS turning colour in the summer heat. And all the hills, like Sir's estate, were now covered with a sheen of gold. They were also dotted with slightly larger brown specks, the sod shacks of the immigrant settlers. As soon as the settlers had arrived, they had begun ploughing—each one with an ox and a single-furrow plough—and planting. Now they too waited impatiently for their first harvest.

Perdue stood on the veranda, looking to the West through Sir's regimental binoculars. He had first spotted the horse and rider when they were only a dark speck in the distant sea of land and heat. They circled around the shacks of the Hussars on the far side of the river, vanished down into the river flats, then rose again, and galloped directly towards the house, smashing a path through the tall, golden grain.

In the round circles of enlarged vision, merging into one, Perdue could now distinguish features quite clearly. The horse's eyes were glazed with exhaustion, his mouth drooling a green froth, his coat a lather of sweat. The man rode bareback, with only a leather bridle to control the animal.

The man was shouting something over and over, his mouth opening wide and closing, opening wide and closing, but Perdue could hear nothing yet. The man was very old. He had long, greasy, grey hair. He wore a ragged buckskin suit, moccasins. He waved a long rifle in his right hand, grasping the bridle with his left.

Perdue took the binoculars from his eyes and the horse and rider became a single dark mass again, becoming slowly larger as they plunged forward on a sea of grain that rippled in the thick, hot air. Perdue began to hear a faint wavering sound. The sound became more distinct, became words.

"They're coming! They're coming!" the man shouted. "They're coming!! They're coming!!"

Perdue raised the binoculars again, scanned the distant horizon. Below the thin blue line of mountains and beyond the shacks across the river, a vast expanse of land seemed to sizzle in his view, as if cooking in the intense force of the high sun. But nothing moved for miles and miles, except the waves of heat, like water burning.

The shouting was louder, "They're coming!! They're coming!!!"

Perdue dropped the binoculars from his eyes. He noticed that Sir had appeared at his side, holding the elephant gun that was almost always in his hands now.

The horse thundered up the rise on the other side of the railway tracks. It stumbled on the rails. Perdue heard two sharp cracks, saw splintered bone emerge from dark hide. The rider was flung headlong onto the earth at the foot of the veranda. The horse, both front legs broken, struggled to rise, screaming horribly. Sir raised his gun and fired. The bullet hit between the animal's eyes, blew off the back of the skull, scattering blood and brains all over its back.

The old man lurched to his knees, blood dripping from his nose. He gazed at Sir with amazingly clear piercing eyes. "Thank God you're here," he said. "The Governor said you would be."

Sir looked at him. "After you've washed up," he said, "you can tell me the whole story." He turned to Perdue. "Show him the trough," he said.

It was true. The old man needed to wash in a way no one Perdue had ever known needed to wash. His buckskin suit and moccasins were stained with gore. Flies crawled all over him. Perdue found it hard to breathe with the smell of the old man so near. He took little sips of the stinking air through pursed lips.

The old man was trembling. "No!" he exclaimed. "No water!! No water!!"

Perdue sat on the veranda at Sir's side. The old man sat far away. The sun slid steadily down the sky. Perdue kept his nose near his tall glass of lemonade. Sir sipped whisky and soda. The old man drank from a bottle, neat. As he told his story, he kept his eyes fixed on the horizon beneath the sun, the way he had come.

"The Governor was my friend," he said. "He knew how valuable I was. I knew what he had to do and I made it easy for him. I knew where all the camps were. I knew how to bring them to him. And I knew how to prepare the welcome.

"One day we camped near the Sandy Hills. The Governor was up before first light, as was his practice, and I rode with him into the hills. He had his easel and paints. He set himself up to do a view of the sand-dunes that formed both sides of a wide valley. They were beautifully rippled by the wind. His surveyors were to measure its depth and width. I remember well, he was drinking his usual tea with brandy in it.

"'Governor,' I said to him. 'I'll go find a camp.'

"'After you've done that,' he said, 'find a place for the meeting and have the troops prepare everything.'

"So I did. I found a camp of about two hundred. Then I came back and showed the soldiers a pretty dell enclosed by steep sand hills on three sides. They were almost cliffs, high as your barn back there. And I showed them how to get things ready.

"The soldiers worked all afternoon and into the evening. They were troubled by the hordes of mosquitoes. The next morning, before dawn, I took a few men with me to fetch the savages.

"We had a bit of trouble right at first, getting them to move in the right direction. But I sent some of my men out to the sides to guide them along, and with others I urged them on from behind. We made them go faster and faster. Finally, they broke and ran.

"Once in a while some tried to veer off, but I had arranged a converging line of gun-pits, in a funnel, and when our soldiers showed themselves and waved their rifles, the savages moved back quickly enough. The funnel narrowed and narrowed, leading them in between the hills to the place we had made ready."

And Perdue's mind dipped into the words of the story like a bucket into well water. And filled. And he was standing at the top of the crescent-shaped hills, looking down at the scene below.

The Indians were running full-out now: men, women, and children trying to escape from the trap. But the pound was waiting: a circular fence set right against the slopes of the hills and dug out at the entrance, so that those running were pitched down into the pound, struggling to evade the fall of others coming after and not always doing so. Perdue could hear limbs breaking, infants being crushed, screams of pain. And then those who could were lurching up and running round and round the fence, strong tree trunks laced together with willow branches and braced with outside supports.

Perdue could see the Governor on a chair above the level of the fence on the slope of the hill, with his easel set to one side and a table with a pile of papers to the other. (Perdue looking down on the Governor's cockade hat, seeing his bright ribbons and his glinting medals catch the morning light.) And one fierce old Chief trying to break through the fence to climb up to the Governor, but the Governor's minor officials jumping up from hiding places behind the fence and waving papers in his face, frightening him back.

The terrified people not knowing which way to turn, shouting and screaming at their captors. The-One-Who-Brings-Them-In moving to the Governor's side, interpreting. The minor officials jumping up and waving papers again and again, and throwing medals with the Queen's face on them, and the people throwing them back, trying to use them as weapons.

The people mad with rage and fear, screaming at the officials. The officials becoming infuriated. The Governor annoyed. Waving a hand at the soldiers, who were hidden behind the fence and closing in from behind. And at once a scene of dreadful confusion and slaughter: a constant din of rifles, the shouts and chanting of the dying, the women baring their breasts, the children moaning.

The agonies of death of so many crowded together furnishing a revolting and terrible spectacle, but with occasional displays of amazing strength and rage as the people flung themselves against the fences, shaking the supports, clawing for the rifles, cursing. Until at last all of them destroyed, lying tossed in every conceivable position of death.

The Governor turning now to his easel to record the sight.

The-One-Who-Brings-Them-In stopped talking.

Perdue opened his eyes. And saw the face of the old man and the face of Sir, bathed with red, as if they were dripping with blood instead of flushed with colour from the setting sun. The-One-Who-Brings-Them-In tipped up the last of the bottle, gulped down crimson fluid.

"Sometimes one or two got away. I know they did. Couldn't be helped. And now the Governor's gone. Sailed away from the West Coast. Going to India. So he told me to come back here to you."

"You'll be safe here," Sir promised.

"Thank you," the old man said. "Thank you very much." He paused, turning his head to look at Sir. "I," he said, "I, too, was a gentleman once."

Perdue, closing his eyes again, choked on the stench of putrefying bodies, and began to push sand, sand, sand down the hill, trying to start a slide of sand to cover the hundreds of corpses, humming and buzzing with millions of large black-blue flies, all feeding on the rotting flesh.

CHAPTER TEN

T HE NEXT TIME the train stopped Sir was ready and waiting. He flung the door open. He spoke.

"Bloody good show! How d'ye do? Have a drink! Jolly good! Have a drink!"

A line of men in morning suits, descending from their carriage, doffed their top hats and shook Sir's hand one after the other. In the lounge, champagne corks popped and the Maid offered the men blown-crystal glasses full of the bubbling liquid. The sideboards bore silver trays heaped with thin slices of pickled buffalo brain on crackers. The new Help, dressed in a crisp white shirt and green-velvet vest and pants, carried the trays around.

Gal Sal languished on a sofa. She wore a flame-coloured tea-gown, a long unshaped sheath of silk, collared, cuffed, and hemmed in ostrich feathers. The dress clung seductively to her otherwise naked body. The men bowed before her, kissing the hand she idly lifted towards them.

"Gentlemen, gentlemen," Sir welcomed them, leaning against the fireplace in a sky-blue crushed-velvet lounging suit. Perdue, dressed in a miniature replica of the same suit, stood beside him. Both of them had prairie lilies pinned to their lapels. "Gentlemen," Sir continued, "show me what you have."

Through the open door, four servants brought in upon their shoulders what looked like a long rug with a wooden pole sticking out at both ends. They laid it on the floor at right angles to the door. Briskly, they cleared chairs and sofas out of the centre of the room.

Returning to the rug, two of them anchored its edges. The other two grasped the wooden pole at its ends and began to unroll it, slowly at first and then faster and faster as the roll of cloth diminished. Behind them spread out an intricate pattern of lines and rectangular shapes sur-rounded by blobs of green. They came closer and closer, finally almost at a run, stopping dead when the last turn of the roll brought it to an end just at the toes of Sir's polished black shoes.

Perdue did not have even a moment to examine the cloth, for through the open door strode yet another man, carrying a gold cane. Perdue blinked his eyes. The man, garbed in a suit of soft cloth the colour of cream, with a jet-black cape trimmed with glossy fur draped from his shoulders, was no taller than Perdue. His face was large and bony, but his body was shrunken, the legs squat.

The man stepped forward onto the cloth, walked to its centre, the cloth crinkling beneath his feet. And there he stopped, bowing to Sir.

Sir clapped his hands, applauding, "Jolly good! Jolly good!" The other men applauded too, vigorously.

The small man waited until they had finished. "Thank you," he said, his voice a gruff squeaking sound. "Thank you most kindly. You see before you," his voice grew louder, "a vision of the future!"

He swung the cane around, indicating the designs on the cloth. "Here we have," he announced, "a Model City for all time to come!" Perdue noticed that "Model City" was indeed written in a wonderfully elegant script right at his feet.

"A symbol of the apotheosis of man's achievements, of the higher ideals of civilization which, in this place, have triumphed over the lower forces of both man and beast!"

The men, enthusiastic, applauded once more.

"The constraint of nature, the restraining influences of education, result in a liberty of expression that may take its shape in the very streets we walk, the buildings in which we live and work, the gardens in which we seek our leisure." He paused, lowering his voice to a compelling whisper. "It lies before you." He swept his cane in a circle. "Look," he commanded. "Look!

"Where I stand," he stamped the tip of the cane, "are the buildings of Government. The centre of all. Like the radiating beams of a star, these wide, boulevarded avenues lead our gaze in. In towards the magnificent structures here, all constructed in the Classical Mode. Surrounded by beautiful formal gardens, the river guided and shaped into reflecting pools, into ornamental canals."

Perdue wondered how this could be done to a creek that overflowed in the spring and shrank to a thin trickle in summer, stagnating and stinking in fall and freezing solid in winter.

The golden cane pointed here and there, following the flow of words. The various features of the design were presented. The First, Second, and Third Class Residential Districts. The wonderful Public Facilities: more parks, with tennis and badminton lawns, a Library, an Art Gallery. Giant Stadia for sports. A vast Fair Grounds for Annual Exhibitions, with buildings for Agriculture, for

Industry, even a Palace of the Arts.

The dwarf looked directly at Sir. "All these gentlemen need," he said, "to turn this Vision of Civilization into Reality, is a small piece of your property on each side of the river, which they would be exceedingly honoured to receive as a donation in token of your Civic Pride and of the position of responsibility and leadership which you hold in this burgeoning community."

The men, turning towards Sir, applauded heartily, saying "Hear! Hear!" with deep, respectful voices.

"Gentlemen, gentlemen," Sir replied. "Absolutely smashing plan! Brilliant conception! Would like nothing more than to help you in every possible way!"

Again the men applauded, even raising a small cheer.

"However," Sir continued. "Sorry to say. Out of my hands . . . quite. Nothing to do with the matter, really."

"What's that?" one of the men exclaimed.

"That flood plain land . . . I say, sorry old chaps, my partners have the final word. You see, my land syndicate sold some shares to some chaps in London—old comrades, bally fellas, looking for a firm investment—and they've sold some of those shares to some Firm or other in the Federal Capital here. Money in the country, what. Sense of National Responsibility."

The men looked downcast.

"Tell you what, though. Good fellows and all. Speak to them for you. Yes, no trouble too much for this magnificent proposal. Put in a good word. Get a good price. For you fellas, bandy-bandy-raggers, do my best! Swear! Old soldiers never die. All the troop. Charge! Clear the way! Tally-ho!!"

The men cheered loudly, clapped their hands, and broke spontaneously into "For He's a Jolly Good Fellow!"

Perdue knew, because he had heard Sir talking with his lawyers (who had arrived and departed the day before), that they had just constructed a long, long chain of Syndicates and Companies and Corporations. And the bits and pieces of the river land would have to be bought from each one in turn, with Sir profiting at every sale.

"Jolly good." Sir was blushing. "Chaps make a fella feel borra-borra. Too awfully good, really."

And Perdue bowed his head, but not before the dwarf had caught his eye and, Perdue was sure, discovered there precisely what he knew.

CHAPTER ELEVEN

PERDUE WAS GROWING, but the wheat was growing too. Now it was nearly as high as the epaulettes on Sir's shoulders when he wore his old uniform. Which meant it was over Perdue's head.

Nonetheless, Perdue loved to walk through the wheat. By putting his shoulders sideways, he could just slip between the rows of stalks, which seemed to go on for ever and ever. And over his head, so that he had to raise his eyes up to them, the billions of grain berries were swelling full with the force of the soil and the sun. Perdue was immersed in a golden world.

Under his bare feet, the warm earth felt soft and yielding. And sometimes Perdue would lie down on his side to peer into the jungle of thin yellow bones, or on his back to be entranced with the heads of grain swaying, swaying, swaying, a dance of gold against blue and white.

He would wander in the fields all day, being caressed by the wheat. And he could feel the power that was in the earth and the light filling him up, surging through him, making him part of the ripening time.

Hungry, Perdue would reach up to the grain, strip the berries from the heads into his hand. Then rub the chaff off and put the berries in his mouth. To chew, releasing their sweet juices, and turning them into a thick, sticky gum.

When the sun set, Perdue could guide himself towards the house by the slant of the rays, which deepened and darkened the colour of the wheat into a burnished golden red.

And sometimes at night, after they had eaten and everyone else had gone to sleep, Perdue would creep through the house and out into the fields again. Under the sheen of the moon the wheat would be gold once more, but a paler gold, as if it were a ghost of itself. And Perdue would move into it and wrap it around himself.

And he would listen to the cry of hunting owls, to the scurry of small creatures who were returning to the blood-stained land, and to the mournful call of coyotes roaming the hills. And, lying down, he would watch the drift of the moon, the ghost of the sun reflected from its pitted face, and the far, far points of dazzling cold fire in the deep black ocean of sky.

CHAPTER TWELVE

BY THE FIRST LIGHT of the rising sun, Perdue, perched high above the hayloft in the lantern of the barn, saw through the binoculars a flurry of activity on the far side of the creek. Men rushed about, driving stakes topped with fluttering coloured ribbons into the earth. Other men consulted large sheets of paper, beckoned in this direction and that. Clumps of workmen holding hammers and saws stood around them. Drivers of teams of horses hitched to wagons full of lumber leaned forward impatiently.

The night before, Perdue had sat with his father in his study. Sir had piles of paper spread out across his desk, and he laughed and laughed as he read them. Land Agents in his control had assisted the Town Fathers in finally purchasing part of the river plain they needed for the town from Sir's assorted Companies, Syndicates, and Corporations. Now the Land Agents, in fact men from Sir's old company of Hussars, on his instructions, were cutting up the land into a grid of streets and cutting up the street blocks into narrow lots. Selling lots in apparent competition, they had driven up the price 2,000 per cent in a week, and were pushing it higher by the minute. Of course, they had already reserved the best sites for themselves.

One of Sir's Companies was also in the contracting business. They had been given the contract to build the town. As the first citizens, scheduled to arrive that evening, got off the train, they would be handed brochures. The brochures said, "Deluxe Residence in an Ideal Location, on a Rise of Land Overlooking the Magnificent River View beyond which the Tremendous Architectural Triumph of New and Spacious Government Buildings Are Soon to Rise!" Then they would be taken to one of the many Real Estate Offices, whichever one they chose, to sign a mortgage. They would be able to move into their new home at once, or stay, if they wished to look around at others, at the Deluxe Rooms in the new Hotel.

All that, Perdue knew, would happen before the day was done. But the town had to be built first.

The army of men set to work. In moments, they knocked down the old shacks in which the Hussars had lived. Then they laid out lines of boards with short planks across them and nailed them down: sidewalks. They pounded together large rectangles of sidewalks, with gaps where the back alleys would go. Into the rectangles they unloaded wagon after wagon of lumber. Then they separated into groups of fifty or so, racing each other to be the first to have a finished structure. They framed, floored, sided, and shingled a house within twenty minutes. They set in windows, put on doors. They uncrated stoves, one for each room, and installed them. Then the crews for plaster and lath moved in.

Meanwhile, the gangs of builders moved across the alley,

framing, flooring, siding, shingling. Doors and windows. Stoves. Streets of houses seemed to explode out of the ground.

Furniture vans, poised outside the dwellings, disgorged themselves into the waiting empty rooms. Rugs first, then chairs, sofas, beds, chests of drawers, wardrobes, kitchen tables, dining-tables, occasional tables, chiffoniers, oil lamps, chandeliers, commodes, dishes, pots and pans, utensils, all flooded into the dwellings.

Through his binoculars, Perdue watched the town rising like buns under a damp cloth. Block after block of houses. Each block a different design. Blocks of two-storey houses with gable windows and screened porches. Blocks of smaller houses with open front porches. The big houses overlooking the stagnant, stinking water. The small houses with views out over the vast prairie.

In between, a Main Street took shape. Real Estate Offices first, with tall, false fronts. A Livery Stable. Dry Goods and Grocery Stores. A couple of Clothing Stores. A Drugstore. A Newspaper. And, at the centre of the street, the three-storey Hotel and Saloon.

The noise of all the hammering and sawing floated faintly on the slow breeze. The sun glared down from almost directly overhead. The men did not stop to eat, they ate as they worked. Building after building was finished and furnished. Perdue went down from his perch and ate a buffalo-roast sandwich and drank some water. He climbed up into the lantern again.

The gangs of men had reached the outskirts of the town. The final houses rose.

The sun slid down the sky.

The train arrived.

The settlers got off.

The sun set.

Lights went on all over town.

CHAPTER THIRTEEN

WHEN PERDUE opened the front door the next morning, the Giant was standing across the railway tracks. He wore two large grey blankets with three red stripes at either end. The blankets were open at the top and bottom, but the sides were laced together with rawhide. The Giant had no shoes or hat. His skin was light brown, his long, tangled hair reddish-black.

On his way to his study, Sir, holding his after-breakfast glass of whisky, stopped behind Perdue. He took one look at the Giant's massive body, his great hands knotted with thick veins, his shoulders broader than any three other men side by side, his impassive, shy face, the eyes downcast. "You can start today," Sir said.

The Giant gave no sign that he heard or understood.

"Back there," Sir gestured with the glass, and walked on.

Behind the house, Sir was having a new mansion built. One of his Companies had the contract for providing the granite and marble from which the new Railway Station and the Government Building would be made. Sir was using some of this stone for his own purposes first. It waited in a line of boxcars on a special siding that ran off at a right angle from the main line in the direction of the town.

The Giant strode towards the back of the house. Perdue followed.

The army of men that had built the town the day before now were busy excavating the basement for Sir's mansion. They had dug out the earth to a depth of two men, one standing on the other's shoulders. They were loading it into wagons and hauling it away to build a dam downstream from the site of the Government Building. The jingle of harness, the plodding of hooves filled the air.

Teams of horses that were not carrying earth for the dam arrived from the boxcars, straining under the granite weight of the heavily loaded stoneboats. Loads of gravel were being taken into the pit and strewn about in an even layer. It was time to start laying the foundations. The men began to wrestle with the stone, trying with levers and ropes to lower it into the pit.

The Giant stepped forward. He moved to the nearest stoneboat. The men stood back, watching intently. The Giant, not even bending his knees, grabbed hold of a huge block of stone. He lifted it easily, lightly, into the air, and jumped down into the pit. He put the stone in a corner and jumped out again. Another stone. Jump down. Jump up. Another stone. Jump down. Up. Another stone. Down. Up. Stone after stone. He emptied the stoneboat before Perdue could release the breath he had gasped in and held.

The stones lay in a straight row from one corner of the excavation to the other. The men, finding their voices again, cheered lustily. The Giant moved to another stoneboat. He emptied it just as quickly.

The masons ran to their mortar troughs. They scraped and slushed the mix to the best consistency. They clambered down ladders into the hole and began filling the cracks between the stones that would soon be a floor.

All that day the Giant worked, lifting stone after stone. And Perdue, sitting first with his legs dangling over the edge of the basement, then further back on the ground, watched. The Giant did not speak. He did not seem to know how to speak, although he understood perfectly what he must do.

The Giant worked. Worked fast enough to keep fifty stonemasons busy, smoothing slurry between the rising layers of stone. Worked fast enough to keep fifty carpenters busy, stringing the joists, nailing floor boards, laying the tongue-and-groove oak floorings. And fifty more framing and installing windows and doors. And two hundred loading granite and marble from the boxcars, bringing it to him with twenty teams of horses.

The Giant worked unceasingly. The basement walls were done. He worked all though the heat of the day. One storey. He did not stop to eat or drink. Two storeys. He did not take off his robe.

The clothes of all the other men were soaked with the effort of trying to keep up to the pace of the Giant. They stripped off their shirts, flung them away. The sweat dripped down their faces and chests, poured from their armpits.

Suddenly Perdue realized that the Giant did not sweat. Perdue moved closer to him. He felt a glow of warmth radiating from the Giant, as if the aura of summer had wrapped itself around him. The Giant lifted enormous block after block of stone. For a long time he had not needed a scaffold, raising the stones high above his head. At length, the carpenters built a ramp, and he used that.

He carried the stones up, dropped them carefully into place with a *chunk!*

But the Giant did not sweat. And he did not smell. Not at all. The men, when they came near Perdue, stank from their exertion and from not enough baths. Perhaps, Perdue thought, the Giant had never been forced to work hard enough to sweat. Was not working that hard even now. Perdue wondered what the Giant's sweat would smell like, or if he ever would have a smell.

CHAPTER FOURTEEN

THE CLOUDS BEGAN to gather in both east and west early one afternoon. They rumbled together, piling up upon one another, tumbling higher and higher into the clear air. Light gave way to dark; blue to black. Slowly the clouds began to move towards the estate, like a vast herd of buffalo rubbing shoulder to shoulder, the thunder of their progress growing ominously in the hush.

The walls of the clouds soared upwards, their tops leaning towards one another until it seemed that they were falling, falling down onto Perdue's head. And then they touched, merged in their highest reaches, forming the swirling roof of a vast cathedral. The floor of the cathedral was all of gold, a gold that pulsed darker and darker as shadows rippled across it in the waning light.

Then the clouds merged lower down as well, grunting

and thundering. Slowly they began to circle, striking long sparks of fire off the surrounding hills. Perdue, in the barn's lantern, turned with their turning, watched them sweep around and around the enormous stretch of swaying wheat, as if trying to suck it up into the whirlpool of their flow.

Upon the hills, the immigrants trembled and prayed, terrified in their sod huts. The stampeding storm smashed down torrents of hail until the rolling shapes of land glistened white, pure white in the brief illumination of blazing flashes. The destruction there was devastating and complete. The mad ghost herd trampled all the crops flat and all the gardens into pulp, leaving only shivering people and dead animals behind.

When it had passed, later that day, those living in the houses of the town would speak of the size of the hail. "As big as goose eggs," one would say. "As big as cabbages," another would reply. "No"—someone else would hold up a hailstone in both hands as they gathered around the dead horses lying in the white streets—"No. As big as prize pumpkins."

"And look over there," they would say, pointing at the great flat plain of Sir's estate. "Not one stalk of that wheat touched. Not one stalk!"

And it was true. The storm had circled and circled, until Perdue knew he was at the dead centre of a spinning stampede of destruction. A frenzied stampede that could not break through the charmed ring of buffalo bone, could not touch the enchanted red-stained earth that nourished the luxuriant life of the wheat.

CHAPTER FIFTEEN

THE PEOPLE WALKED out of their sod huts, across the hills, and along the railway tracks to reach Sir's front door. Men carrying newly sharpened scythes. Men wearing rough, home-made jackets, trousers, and boots. Men laying their scythes down and clenching dark, sweat-stained caps and hats in both hands. Men bowing heads. And women behind them in long, dark dresses, with brightly patterned kerchiefs over braided hair.

Sir, after breakfast, went straight out the door, across the tracks—the mass of people parting to let him pass—and into the wheat. Perdue followed. Sir grasped a hand around a couple of stalks, slid it up, stripping the berries from the heads. He rubbed his hands together, removing the chaff, blew it off the grain.

The berries were plump and creamy white. Sir squeezed

one between his thumb and fingers. Earlier in the week, when he had done this, a small, clear drop of liquid had emerged. Now there was no moisture. The wheat was flinty, fully hardened, and completely ripe.

Sir turned and strode back to the veranda. He faced the throng of people whose own crops had been destroyed by the storm. While his was unbelievably whole and was certain to yield more than one hundred bushels to the acre.

Sir did not raise his voice. "Fifty cents a day," he said quietly, "for the men. Ten cents for the women."

Men just out of range of Sir's voice were told the offer by their neighbours and the word passed through the crowd. Reached its farthest edges. Then something began moving back. Reached the man standing right in front of Sir. He did not speak, simply bowed his head very low.

"Good," said Sir. "Start now."

Stooping, almost as one, the men picked up their scythes from the ground. They turned to confront the wheat.

During the two weeks that it took to reap the grain, Perdue got used to seeing the long, long line of men, dark shapes slowly cutting their way through a bright barrier. Their scythes, sweeping gracefully in strong arcs, shimmered in the sun. And behind the men, the women gathered the fallen grain into bundles and formed it carefully into stooks, nine sheaves to each stook.

Perdue knew that, although there was much respect— even awe—in the way the people treated the grain, there was also an immensity of feeling he could not quite define. It was like a profound sadness, but was not quite sadness either. This was what the land could do, Perdue saw them thinking, this richness, this marvellous harvest. It could do this. But it had not done it for them. How could it be made to do it for them? How?

The days were hot. The people worked hard, walking

out of the hills at sunrise and only returning to their homes at sunset. Sir rode out during the day on Stud, surveying their progress and eyeing the women.

The work on the outside of the new mansion had been completed. Now plasterers, wood carvers, and painters were inside. The rest of the army of builders, and the Giant, had built the new Railway Station and then begun to excavate and lay the foundations for the Government Building.

At the end of the day, Perdue would stand on the veranda, looking towards the building site. And he would watch the figure of the Giant striding across the fields stripped of grain, fields full of stooks, as if he were emerging from the low, burning disc of the setting sun. His figure would grow larger and larger until Perdue could not see the sun itself, only the Giant surrounded by a glowing halo of fiery light.

When the wheat was all cut and stooked, the people returned to where they had begun. They gathered up the first stooks, now dry and ready for threshing. The men piled stooks on the bent backs of the women, and they carried them in from the fields to the area around the barn where the Percherons had been driven in circles, day after day, to pack down the earth.

There, several rings of men surrounded the wheat, and with flails beat the grain loose from the chaff. The women threw stook after stook into the rings, until at last the men would stop, step away, and form a new ring. Into the old ring the women brought large, flat, woven baskets. They piled in the grain, then threw it into the air, letting the wind winnow the chaff from the grain, which they caught in the baskets again. Then they cleared the chaff away, carrying it out beyond the new house, forming great piles of chaff that soon reached in an enormous circle all around the buildings.

On the spur line, the boxcars—emptied of stone—stood waiting to receive the grain. The people filled up sacks. They carried them on their backs to the boxcars. They dumped them out into the cars, putting planks across the open door of each car as the grain covered the floor and rose higher and higher. They took the empty sacks back, filled them again, carried them, dumped them. The cars quickly became packed with grain.

A locomotive came, pulling another long line of empty boxcars. It took away those that were full. The new cars were filled. The locomotive came with more. They were filled.

The harvest of the land poured through their hands and into the hands of more of Sir's Companies, grain agents, grain speculators. People were hungry, people needed bread. And a silver flood of coins poured forth from pockets so that some small part of the golden river of grain could trickle into waiting, into open mouths.

CHAPTER SIXTEEN

WHEN PERDUE walked out of the front door after breakfast, the train was right there, more than fifty cars stopped, closing off the main line. Perdue ducked underneath a carriage. On the other side, hundreds of men bustled about, unloading thousands of bundles.

A dozen teams of horses, attached to ploughs, were turning under the stubble field in front of the house. Other teams pulled wide, weighted bars to smooth the soil, and still others pulled massive, cylindrical rollers to pack the earth down. Upon the firm, flat surface that had been created, workmen unrolled rug after rug, covering the dusty earth with intricate patterns of trees and flowers and animals and birds in bright colours. They laid down hundreds of rugs, thousands of rugs, carefully overlapping their edges, until acres of land were transformed.

Close to the train, other workmen unfurled sections of

canvas striped blue and red and yellow. They laced the sections together. They drove wooden pegs right through the rugs, deep into the earth. They raised tall wooden poles. They lifted the canvas up with ropes and pulleys into an enormous square tent. And they shinnied up the poles to place streamers and flags at their tops.

Finishing that, they took from the train the gleaming segments of a giant wooden puzzle. They carried them away from the train, out into the centre of the area of rugs. Then again they unfurled canvas, drove pegs, raised poles, and lifted another pavilion tent—this time circular in shape—over a polished circular floor.

At the same time, the stonemasons, who had worked on Sir's new house and now were working on the Government Building, began to construct a bridge to pass over the train. The bridge grew a supporting arch, then walls pierced with panes of leaded glass, and decorated with naked figures of stone, with clusters of stone fruit and flowers. The bridge grew a roof, covered with tiny cupolas. One of the workmen engraved some words into the stone at one side of the bridge. Perdue understood the letters, but not how they combined into such strange patterns. Then the workman cut more words into the other side of the bridge. "Bridge of Sighs," Perdue read. "Venice."

All of the teams of horses, all the workmen stopped. They had finished. They returned to the train.

Perdue walked across the rugs, walked out to the pavilion with the glistening floor. The morning sun, beating upon the coloured canvas, filled the pavilion with golden, turquoise, and crimson light. On a raised platform at the far end was something which Perdue, who had been watching the building of the bridge, had not seen the workmen carry in. It looked like a very large, curving box, made of gleaming black wood. It balanced on three solid, carved legs. A cover on the top was propped open. A bench was placed at one end, before a row of white.

Perdue stepped up onto the platform. The inside of the box was filled with wires strung closely together. Perdue saw that the row of white had segments, and separate black pieces raised above. He placed his left hand on the row of white and black and pressed down softly. The segments moved down, lifted up when he removed his hand. He pushed down harder.

The silent space, the glowing coloured air, reverberated with dark, throbbing sounds.

Upon the motionless patterns of carpet moved a host of men and women. The women wore elegant dresses, delicate lace and pastel silk draped in swirls about them, trailing on the ground. White gloves reaching up above their elbows. Large hats of finely woven straw topped with froths of feathers that trembled as they turned or nodded their heads. They carried parasols with handles of silver. Jewels glittered from brooches pinned to bosoms, from pendants hanging on fragile gold chains, from clusters of rings on fingers.

Some of the men—once Hussars, but now respectable citizens of the town—had worn their old uniforms. Lustrous black boots, scarlet breeches, purple- and black-velvet jackets, gold braid. With one arm, each one cradled a silver helmet topped with white plumes. Rapiers hung at their sides. In deference to the heat, they had not worn their blood-red capes.

Other men wore black morning coats with long tails of dark cloth dangling down over pin-stripe trousers. They carried top hats tucked in the crooks of arms.

Waiters hovered discreetly near, balancing glasses full of champagne on trays, or trays heaped with tidbits. They offered the food and drink at the merest beckoning gesture of a finger.

Perdue, who had just been dressed by the Maid in a miniature version of the Hussar's uniform, a small rapier at his side, stepped off the Bridge of Sighs. He turned south, walking along beside the train, past the coal car, past the locomotive, towards the distant edge of the rugs. He did not want to be part of that crowd whose idle conversations melted together into a humming drone in the clear prairie air. He did not want to be any closer to Gal Sal's tinkling laughter, to Sir's guffaws.

At the edge of the rugs he stopped and looked at a big rectangular field of packed earth which had been outlined in chalk. At the east and west ends of the field, pairs of white posts, quite close together, had been set into the ground. Perdue walked near the fringes of the rugs, taking care not to step off into the dust of the beaten earth and smudge his shining boots.

Reaching the south-west corner of the rug-covered area, Perdue turned north. A long row of horses, attached to carriages and tethered to drinking troughs, lifted dripping muzzles and turned their heads to watch Perdue as he passed. Their large eyes were placid, untroubled. Strings of more spirited ponies, tied to the last of the troughs, whinnied and pranced.

Perdue turned right again at the next corner, walking past boxcars filled with grain and boxcars being filled. On the other side of the cars, out of sight of the festivities, the people worked, carrying sacks of grain, dumping the last of the harvest into the waiting cars. Perdue could see their worn boots underneath the train, could hear them murmuring to each other in languages he did not understand.

To his right, the new train loomed up. Perdue turned again, completing the square, and went past the caboose and past boxcars from which the rugs and pavilions had emerged. He came to a number of closed-in cars with smoke issuing from stovepipes in a row on their roofs. The cars pulsed with heat. From inside them, Perdue heard the rattling of metal and muted shouts.

He reached the pavilion he had not been in. There were

open doors in the rear canvas wall. Perdue stepped inside.

Table after table had been joined together to form a great hollow square. The tables were laid with snow-white cloths and were set with silver cutlery, with porcelain plates, with crystal goblets. All this Perdue took in at a glance. But what he did not expect, what made him pause and stare, was an enormous block of ice, taller than three men one on top of the other, set right in the middle of the square formed by the tables.

A man stood high on a trestle which surrounded the ice, holding a wooden mallet and a chisel. He worked rapidly, chipping away at the ice. It fell in scintillating sprays, landing silently on the brilliant patterns of the rugs.

The man must have been at work for some time, for Perdue already saw vague forms emerging from the blue-white depths of the ice. He shivered suddenly from the chill hanging in the air and backed quickly out the door.

Horses, running at full gallop, jostled together, nearly throwing their riders off. The men shouted, reining the horses abruptly around, madly dashing off in another direction. Dust billowed into the air. One horse went down. The rider rolled off. He got to his feet, dazed, bleeding from the nose.

Upon the rugs on one side of the playing field, ladies lounged on folding canvas chairs, twirling their parasols to ward off the scorching rays of the late afternoon sun. Gentlemen leaned over them, pointing out a good play, a fine shot. The pounding of hooves, the shouts of command and fierce exhortation, the chunk of wooden mallets on the wooden ball clamoured through the air.

The ball sailed between the wooden goal-posts. A burst of triumphant cheers rose up. The players cantered their horses to the sidelines. The spectators applauded enthusiastically.

Sir leapt down off Stud, throwing the reins to a groom.

It was Perdue's duty to hold a towel ready for his father, Gal Sal's to have a glass of cold punch waiting. Sir handed Perdue the polo mallet. With the towel he wiped away the sweat that dripped from his face, leaving streaks of mud. He took off his pith helmet and rubbed the back of his neck, at the same time picking up and draining the glass of cold liquid.

"Bloody good show," he announced. "Fast chukka. Bloody fast."

The other players dismounted and were handed towels and glasses of punch. They listened attentively to Sir.

"Jolly bash-up! Bandog and Bedlam! Pukka fella did a barney, pushed him off, borra wallah came a cropper!"

All the players laughed, even the one who had fallen.

"Chopped over near side! Slammed it back! Bandy ragger show! Short leathers, short leathers! Chukka time! Borra-borra chukka!!"

The players cheered, mounted up on fresh ponies held by the grooms. Sir waved off another horse and got back on Stud, who reared and turned, eager for the sport. They raced out onto the grounds, formed opposing lines. A servant threw the ball between and the game began again.

And all along the railway track at the eastern end of the playing field, attracted by the tumult, the harvesters gathered, faces burned dark by the sun. They stood impassive, silent, watching.

The banquet table was finally clear of food. They had eaten vichyssoise, crème d'épinard, consommé, and carrot soup; had consumed stewed eels, sole filets, cod filets, red mullet, smoked salmon, pickled herring, crab and crayfish, lobster claws, and whole stuffed trout; had dispatched garnished tongue, boiled ham, leg of lamb, roast beef, rabbit stew, steak and kidney, braised veal, and a brace of roast suckling pigs; had gnawed on cold birds, snipe and pheasant, duck and quail, goose and turkey, pigeon pie;

had swallowed cold aspic, spiced bread, stuffed truffles, heaping bowls of vegetables and rice; had devoured charlotte russe, maids of honour, pear mould, plum pudding, apple pie, cream pie, pêches Melbas, soufflés, pommes à la Condé, chocolate mousse, fresh fruit, trays of cheese; had guzzled champagne, claret, rosé, blanc de blancs, and now were sipping brandy (the ladies sipping port) with cigars and with coffee and with tea.

Perdue had taken very little. Plates overflowing with food had been placed in front of him again and again, but he had scarcely noticed. He had been watching the images of ice, watching them melt.

At the start of the feast, the air in the pavilion had been chill. And the figures in the ice, fashioned in precise and startling detail, had loomed up significant and powerful. A massive buffalo, its head lowered as if to charge, one hoof scraping the earth angrily. And, on either side, an Indian man and woman. The woman held a child, suckling at her breast. The man had on a magnificent feather head-dress. Otherwise they were quite naked.

Now the banquet had ended. The figures had vanished, transformed by the heat of the food and the press of bodies into insubstantial, featureless mounds. The meltwater trickled down, soaking the rugs, and seeping under the tables, moistening the shoes and boots of those who sat there.

Perdue lay back in one of the folding canvas chairs that were still strewn about. A full harvest moon hung bright in the star-sprinkled sky. He looked at the round pavilion. The striped canvas glowed from the lamps inside. Massive shadows moved upon its surface, a mad jumble of whirling shadows. He heard the slide and shuffle of capering feet. And he heard sounds he had never heard before.

The low throb of deep notes, the sweet flow of a piercing melody, and, holding both together, blending high and low, violin and bass fiddle, the rhythmic syncopation of the big black instrument. Perdue did not want to see how these sounds were produced; it was enough that they existed, that their harmonious urging of these hundreds of people into a whirl of motion could turn them into flat dark shapes upon the tent walls.

And watching this dance of the shades, the music a faint tremor soon lost in the vast empty space of prairie, of night sky, Perdue slipped into sleep.

The next morning, everything—pavilions, rugs, the Bridge of Sighs, the train, even the boxcars of grain—everything was gone.

CHAPTER SEVENTEEN

THE LINE shuffled forward. Each one bent to make a mark on paper, then received the money, crisp, brand-new bills. Eight dollars for sixteen days of harvest work, plus $1.60 for a woman's work.

The smell of roast meat was almost unbearably strong. Perdue's mouth kept filling up with saliva, which he spat out as the men did, wiping their mouths on the backs of thick, dark hands.

To provide for the feast, they had carried the carcasses up from the ice-house that was nestled deep into the earth and protected inside the arms of the old house. Perdue had followed the men down the sloped runway to the door. Sir led the way, carrying a lantern that burned almost invisibly in the bright morning air. He stood aside while the men moved the layers of hay away from the door.

The door swung open, releasing a chill gust of air. Sir went in. The men crowded in after him, hiding the lantern from Perdue's sight. It was as if they had vanished into the dark. Then Sir began to light other lamps that hung from the beams.

Perdue saw a long, gleaming corridor open before them as the lamps began to glow. Blocks of ice were piled on both sides, carved into an arc high overhead. The men moved along the corridor, following Sir, deep into the intense cold. Perdue swung the door shut behind him. Shivering, he walked after the men, his feet sinking into the thick, spongy layer of sawdust that covered the earth. The air was completely motionless, the sounds of the moving men deadened. They disappeared from sight.

From the central corridor, others ran off on both sides at right angles. Sir had led the men to the farthest one. Perdue, reaching the one nearest the door, glanced along it to the right, saw what the men would have seen when they turned.

Bodies. A long row of bodies. Cut in halves. Suspended from beams. Hung on large metal hooks.

Perdue looked back to the left. More bodies, their glistening flesh, stripped of its skin, mottled, creamy-white and red in the light of the hissing lanterns. Bodies fading into darkness the lanterns could not overwhelm.

There were more than fifty corridors branching off from the main avenue of ice. All of them full with hundreds upon hundreds of these silent artefacts of a vanished past. The first harvest to be taken from the land.

The people were not happy. Their bellies were swollen with roasted meat, gurgling with home-made wine. They wanted to dance, but the sun was going down and the fire in the roasting pits had died to embers. Already the shadows had lengthened to unrecognizable shapes and the brilliant colours of the sunset had faded and then darkened into murky depths. The moon, the overturned blade of a sickle, was a thin, pale, too-distant light.

Yet the earth where they had beaten the grain free from its hulls was smooth, perfect for twirling, for leaping, for the spinning motions of the fire in the blood to be released. The fiddles were jostling, glissandos gliding off one another in the quiet air, high and low notes held and falling away or soaring up into melody.

Perdue wanted the people to dance. To dance the completion of harvest. To dance the defiance of winter. A dance to remember when they were locked in their sod huts by the deep snow and bitter cold. Shivering in their sleep, and dreaming, even when awake, of what their land might give to them next year.

Sir had gone into the house long ago, to work in his study. He had paid the people and given them a feast. He did not care to give them anything more. He did not care if they danced.

Perdue took a long piece of wood from the scrap pile near the new house. He carried it to a roasting pit and stuck it in the coals at the edge until it was burning steadily. Then, holding it high over his head, he ran out past the barn, out past the new stone mansion, out into the fields. The stubble, sharp as arrowheads, lanced his naked feet. Perdue reached the first of the towering piles of chaff that lay in a great circle all around the buildings. He thrust his torch into it.

The chaff exploded into flames that leapt upwards into a pillar of light. Perdue raced on. He set the next mound of chaff alight. And the next. Then the Giant was beside him, sweeping him up onto his shoulders. Perdue felt the summery warmth of the Giant's body engulf him. Then they were running as Perdue had never run before, faster and faster around the circle of chaff piles.

And they ran from the roar of the strengthening fires until the torch was burned down to a stump that scorched

Perdue's hand. But now the world was full of light, and the fiddles raced into the dance. The men and women spun around and around, laughing and shouting.

Walking back towards the music and the noisy and whirling figures, the Giant stopped by the barn. He lifted Perdue down from his shoulders. And Perdue saw, in the enormous eyes that were now low enough for him to look into, large tears glistening, then falling, tear after tear, until they fell in a stream down the vast cheeks of the Giant.

Perdue went into the barn and climbed up to the lantern. From there he watched as the burning piles of chaff, igniting the stubble, joined in a true circle of fire. And the circle began to eat its way out into the fields, widening and widening. A receding wall of flames that released into the air a pungent and rich odour, the final surrender of the dry, red earth. And the nearer piles of chaff were pillars of blazing light that burned and burned and burned until they scorched their image on Perdue's eyes for an everlasting time, so that even as he closed them, not knowing that he closed them, his eyes still saw enormous shapes of fire.

CHAPTER EIGHTEEN

IT WAS NOT the pale light of an October dawn that woke Perdue. It was the smell.

It should have been the smell of burned earth, stretching out charred and ashen to the boundaries of bone, to the fire-guard that had been hastily ploughed to protect the Government Building. The smell of blackened earth upon which nothing moved, which was absolutely empty of any form of human or other life. The harvesters had left during the night, passing along the railway tracks that bridged the scorched land, going home to their sod huts.

Perdue stood up, sniffing the calm, chill air, looking out upon the land below. And his nostrils filled with a strange, keen fragrance, compounded of wild grasses flowing in a warm breeze, of wild flowers surging up to a spring sun, prairie roses bursting open, of blossoms on chokecherry, buffalo berry, saskatoon bushes, the leaves of wolf willow.

An overwhelming smell exactly like that which had washed over him not so long ago, when they had first arrived on the prairie and the land was bubbling with renewed life, ducks on all the sloughs, meadow larks and crows winging overhead, the earth green and watery, buffalo, deer, and innumerable smaller creatures roaming freely.

Turning, dropping to his knees, Perdue started to lift the trapdoor over the ladder that led down into the hay-loft. And the astounding fragrance exploded up into his face, dizzying all his senses with its intensity. With both hands holding the trapdoor partly open, Perdue paused, astonished at a marvellous sight.

Held in the golden chunk of light that came slanting through one of the octagonal windows at the eastern end of the barn, the Giant was stretched out on the hay. Beside him, still in shadow, a woman stood. Falling to her knees, Gal Sal entered the light. She touched the Giant's chest, caressed his belly. Shifting, she grasped the lower edge of his blanket robe and began to lift it up, revealing his enormous knees, his mighty thighs, and, finally, a massive, swelling cock. As Perdue watched, the cock rose higher and higher, until it was as long as Stud's when he mounted a mare. The cock trembled and pulsed.

Gal Sal lifted her dress up, over her smooth, white shoulders, over her head with its flowing blonde hair. She threw the dress on the hay. Then she took off her petticoat and camisole, exposing all of her body to the view of the Giant. Her hair fell down, curling upon her breasts, her back. Perdue, who had seen this body before, was still intrigued by its shapes and motions.

She stepped one foot delicately across the Giant's belly, straddling his body, turning to face him. Then she began to lower herself, moving her crotch closer and closer to the towering cock. Reaching down with both hands, Gal Sal grasped the cock, guiding it to her. She rocked back and forth, slowly back and forth, trying to ease it inside. She began to whimper. And the Giant started to groan, a rumbling, unceasing groan.

And Perdue closed his eyes, so that he could concentrate more completely on the odour that Gal Sal, looking out over the prairie that first time, had lamented they would never smell again. A wild fragrance that soaked into every part of Perdue's being, that surged through him with such a passionate sharpness that he hardly heard the whimpering, groaning screams of ecstasy that throbbed through the barn, disturbing the animals in their stalls below, and perhaps even echoing faintly in the ears of all those lying in their beds in the far hills and in the town.

CHAPTER NINETEEN

THE SKY WAS a blank, burning blue. Powdery black ash covered the earth. Behind Perdue, a trail of dark puffs hovered in the hot, thick air as he walked towards the Government Building.

The new mansion with the copper roof was finished, outside and in. Perdue had gone there first, up the spiral staircase to the second floor, up through the attic with its stained-glass gable windows, up the ladder through a trap-door, and out. Onto a flat, six-foot square of copper with an ornamental railing all around, and a lightning-rod jabbing thinly into the sky. This look-out, Perdue found, was exactly on a level with the lantern in the barn.

Then he had wandered through the house, absorbing its odours of fresh plaster and wood shavings, its double-paned, leaded windows, its pale oak floors gleaming with new varnish, its mahogany woodwork and doors, its elegant spaces, its cellar pantries packed with all manner of supplies, its multitude of rooms, making all these things familiar, making them his own.

Now the Giant was at work on the Government Building. He carried stone after stone up switchback wooden ramps to where the masons worked at the top of the walls, trowelling a slurry of mortar into place. On the back and side walls of the great structure, the workmen used pulleys and slings to lift the stones. But the wall the Giant supplied was rising faster.

At night the Giant still returned to sleep in the hayloft. And there, very often, early in the morning, to be visited by Gal Sal.

Perdue walked around to the front of the building. On the ground before it, a group of men bent over huge slabs of stone, laid out side by side. With hammers and a variety of steel chisels, they carved intently, working from a model of the building, in which a panorama of figures was positioned directly above the wide stone steps that led up to the front entrance. At the moment, the staircase was in place, and the supporting columns. Perdue saw that the men had nearly finished their work, and he knew that it would soon be hoisted up and joined together.

The men had carved deeply into the surface of the stone, bringing forth an interwoven panoply of startlingly realistic shapes. At the very centre of the design, an enormous ox, entwined with chains of flowers, allowed itself to be led by these frail strands. A woman, clad in flowing robes that bared one breast, held the halter of flowers in one hand. In the other she raised a book aloft. She peered intently forward, ignoring both book and beast. Clustering around, figures of men in top hats and morning coats looked admiringly up at her. They carried rolls of paper and surveying instruments. On either side of them, farther away from the woman and the submissive animal, men in rougher clothes clutched sheaves of grain, and women in plain dresses carried baskets of fruit. Intricate and interlocking geometrical designs—triangles, circles, squares—surrounded the entire composition.

Perdue left the men to their carving. He walked over to an enormous single wedge of granite, balancing upon its narrower end, and set apart from the great pile of stone blocks. Sitting down in its shade, Perdue watched the Giant work. The Giant hoisted block of stone after block of stone, holding each of them straight out in front of his body as he moved up the ramps. The Giant did not stop for a breath, he did not cease his efforts. He lifted and carried the ponderous stones as if they were so many bales of hay.

It was an extraordinarily hot day. It seemed as if a day from the middle of July had hidden somewhere, only now coming out and pushing aside what should have been pleasantly cool October weather. If Perdue had not placed himself in the shadow, he would have been scorched by the heat of the glaring sun.

Yet the Giant, draped with the thick folds of the trade blankets, did not sweat. His body, radiating a summery warmth, nonetheless looked cool. His forehead was smooth and dry.

Behind him, across the creek, Perdue knew that the town was sweltering. That people were sheltering inside their homes, the hotel, the bar, gasping for breath and fanning themselves. And the ornamental lake, which had filled up soon after the dam was in place, was now almost totally dry. Stagnant pools of murky water shrivelled, leaving behind deeply fissured, bone-dry mud.

The Giant, unconcerned, worked on. Drowsy, Perdue leaned against the stone, looking at the fossilized remains of creatures that once lived in the warm, tropical sea that had long ago covered the land. He became entranced with tracing their forms with his fingers.

The Giant touched Perdue's shoulder, waking him. He

pointed to the single, massive block of stone against which Perdue rested. It was the keystone for the entire dome that now rose over the roof of the building. It tapered in slightly on all sides at the bottom, forming a huge wedge that would lock all the other stones in place.

Perdue wanted to go up on the Building, wanted to look out over the prairie from that height. He pointed to the top of the stone, and the Giant held out a hand for Perdue to step on, hoisting him smoothly up.

Then the Giant, bending down, placed his hands on either side of the stone block. He pressed up. Slowly. The massive wedge of stone, with Perdue standing on top, glided evenly into the air. The Giant, lifting it straight over his head, shifted his palms under the base of the stone and curled his fingers up on two of its sides. Then he began to carry it up the ramps.

Perdue tipped his head, looked up at the men on top of the completed wall, who had stopped to stare in amazement at what the Giant was doing. They called to the workmen on the other walls, who ran over to see. Even the carvers looked up from their work, astonished. Along the top of the wall, with a space in the middle for the Giant to move through, was a long line of men, human gargoyles leaning over to keep their eyes on what was happening below.

And, thus transfixed, none of them saw the tornado blast through town, exploding through its flimsy buildings in the flash of an instant. And, thus transfixed, none of them saw the twisting, dark shape coming their way until they felt the first whip of wind slash across their faces.

The men had no time at all to react to the quick leap of the funnel as it skipped across the dry lake and touched down at the precise centre of the top of the front wall at the exact moment when the Giant was taking the final step onto the roof.

GEOFFREY URSELL
78

The funnel did not touch the line of men; it did not touch the wall, the roof, the dome. It simply picked up the Giant, with the huge keystone still hoisted high over his head, Perdue balancing there, exhilarated with the view towards the hills, and whirled them into the air.

Perdue waited for what he thought was a thick storm of dust to pass. He had the sensation of floating, although he did not know why. The stone he stood on was quite still, but all around him, so close they almost touched the sides of the rock, an encircling wall of wind, thick with dust and splintered boards, madly spun and spun with relentless, dizzying force. Perdue could not see at all beyond that wheeling darkness.

And then the massive stone fell, plummeting straight down, Perdue transfixed and unmoving, standing on it. The tornado drove the stone down through the air, smashing it into the earth with enormous force, and lifting away from it once more.

Perdue found himself standing, his feet on the level of the grass, in front of the new stone house. Sir, field-glasses held to his eyes, looked out over Perdue's head towards the town. The-One-Who-Brings-Them-In and Gal Sal stood beside him.

Something fell from the sky down through Perdue's vision, and he involuntarily reached out his hand and grabbed it. It was warm and wet at one end. He held his hand up, palm open. He had caught a finger, severed just above the knuckle which should have attached it to a huge hand.

Gal Sal stepped forward, paused. Her face was blank with shock, her eyes wide and staring. Then she flung herself at Perdue's feet, weeping uncontrollably, her lips pressed to the rock, her tears forming a pool on the un-melting stone.

The-One-Who-Brings-Them-In sauntered over to Perdue. "I saw him smiling," he said. "I caught a glimpse right at the end. Even as that stone drove him into the ground. Just like a hammer on a spike." He noticed what Perdue was holding, picked the finger up, and examined it. "The bones in these would make a very nice necklace," he said. "Do you want it? He was your friend."

Perdue looked at him, unthinking. He nodded.

"Be a terrible time trying to find them. Scattered every which way. But I'll get them for you." He got down on his hands and knees, combing through the long grass, plucking fingers from it.

Sir lowered his field-glasses. "Didn't touch the Government Building," he announced, "but the bloody town's gone." He began to laugh.

"Bloody marvellous! Bloody, bloody marvellous!! Must get the word out double quick. Telegrams. TERRIBLE DISASTER! PROPERTY DAMAGE IN MILLIONS!! GOVERNMENT AID URGENTLY NEEDED!!!"

Sir laughed so hard that tears streamed down his cheeks. And Gal Sal, who had been grieving helplessly, had wept so hard that she had no more tears to shed. She stared at Sir with eyes as dry and hard as old bone.

CHAPTER TWENTY

THERE WAS no moon, there were no stars. The layer of cloud was thick and low. The charred earth merged with pitch-black air. In the lurid world of night, all dimensions had been lost. When he looked up for the sky, down to the ground, out to the hills, Perdue saw only darkness visible. Not sky, nor ground, nor hills. Nor even hands held at arm's length away from eyes.

Yet Perdue, turning around, saw a row of gleaming squares of brilliant light floating in the darkness. Within these squares he saw the sheen of highly polished wood, African cormandel, Circassian walnut, rosewood from Brazil, and the rich weave of cloth of gold, cloth of silver, velvet, silk, and satin. Figures, resplendent in red touched with gold and purple, moved through the squares, disappearing, reappearing, disappearing. Moving to and from the central blocks of lustrous radiance, where Sir, in full-dress uniform, and Gal Sal, in low-cut silvery gown, were finishing their meal in the dining-car of the Royal Train, in the presence of His Highness Most Serene.

The Royal Tour had paused that morning. The new town had been scheduled to receive a speech and an inspection. Now there was no town. So His Highness Most Serene had visited Sir. They had gone riding in the hills, had played billiards in the old house, had shot prairie chicken in the valley farther down the creek, had been drinking since three in the afternoon, eating since seven. They were still drinking and eating. It was midnight.

Perdue lay on the ground. He had watched the servants carry Sir out of the railway carriage after Sir had fallen face forward onto his fifth serving of Black Forest torte. Gal Sal and His Highness were alone. Alone, that is, with thirty servants standing silently around the dining-room, watching every movement of His Highness on the chance that one movement or casual word might really be a command.

Suddenly the servants were all leaving, disappearing, reappearing, disappearing, into rooms where curtains were drawn. And His Highness Most Serene was scrabbling at his clothes, ripping them off his drooping chest, his fat, floppy belly, beneath which was scarcely visible the Majestic and erect Royal cock, no larger than a silver coffee spoon. Frantically, he swept the table clear of plates and glasses and Black Forest torte, so that Gal Sal could lower herself back upon the cloth. She began to raise her long dress, sliding it up above her ankles, above her knees, her thighs. His Highness Most Serene watched intently, and Perdue saw the Majestic cock begin to dribble a few thick drops of fluid, then droop and shrivel. Neither of them had touched the other, nor did it seem that they would.

Perdue got up from the cold ground. He was tired. He walked parallel to the train and then cut in a wide circle that led him past the barn to the new stone house, where he had moved some buffalo robes for a bed, in advance of the others. The house was perfectly still. Perdue nestled down in the robes and, all alone, slept.

In the morning, the Royal Train was gone. So were Gal Sal, the Maid, and the new Help. Sir was snoring in a sodden stupor that Perdue did not disturb.

CHAPTER TWENTY-ONE

WHEN THE Indians at last arrived, they took The-One-Who-Brings-Them-In by surprise. He was in the barn, pitching hay to the Percherons. The Indians were at his back before he realized they were there. Pretending not to have seen them, he kept on pitching hay, making his plans.

Then all at once he whirled, leaping in the same motion, and thrusting the razor-sharp tines of the pitchfork into the man just below the ribs. The tines passed through, out the man's back, and drove deep into one of the pine posts that supported the beams. For a moment they all stood transfixed, The-One-Who-Brings-Them-In, the Indian man, the woman, and the small girl child who was holding the woman's hand. And Perdue, who had just climbed down from the loft after watching the Royal Train cut through the distant northern hills, going back the way it had come, its whistle screeching triumphantly.

Then the man screamed. The-One-Who-Brings-Them-In tried to pull out the pitchfork, but the wood had too strong a hold. Releasing it at once, he pulled a long knife from his pouch. The woman dropped the girl's hand, pulling her own skinning knife free from its sheath. She leapt at The-One-Who-Brings-Them-In, and although he caught her on the way, she also had a chance to drive her blade low into his belly, ripping up with all her force, as if she were tearing open the belly of a wild beast. They dropped beside each other, groaning. The man, his eyes still open, breathing·in quick, gurgling gasps, slumped down, supporting his upper body on the handle of the pitchfork.

The girl stood quietly, suddenly alone and lost in a strange world. She had only known these two people, always staying away from the cultivated fields and the sod huts of the settlers. They had travelled up and down the creek valley in the night, camping in caves dug below the valley rim, and returning time and time again to the terrible place where the tribe had been swallowed up by the wave of blood.

She was the love child. The child conceived on that night of the flood of death. The child through whose destiny this event might be comprehended and dealt with. The naked child, whose only adornment was a round moon shape, woven of porcupine quills dyed yellow, hanging from her neck.

Perdue climbed down from the loft. He took the child by the hand and led her away from this completion of the slaughter of the past. He let go of her hand only to swing shut the barn doors. Then, grasping her warm touch once more, he led her into the new house, the stone house made by the Giant, and gave her bread with honey.

CHAPTER TWENTY-TWO

PERDUE WATCHED Sir stumble across the yard. Sir had seen there was no train. Now he was on his way to the barn, probably to saddle Stud and ride after them.

Sir carried his elephant gun in one hand and a belt of cartridges in the other. He still wore his full-dress uniform, a row of medals dangling from his chest. But the medals did not gleam, and the uniform was all smudged with the dried remains of Black Forest torte. Perdue could hear that Sir was screaming curses at the top of his lungs, because the curses were quite audible, even through the double-pane glass window.

When Sir had nearly reached the barn, Perdue turned away from the window. He left the child eating bread. She had honey spread all over her face, and she was smiling. Perdue slipped out of the new house and, hidden from

Sir's view now, raced for the back of the barn.

Sir went into the barn. He shouted. "Bloody hell!!" Then Perdue heard two immense explosions. The terrified scream of horses. A pause. Another shot. Now Perdue was at the barn wall. He looked in through an open knot-hole.

At three headless corpses. At Sir, saying "Bloody pack of savages." At Sir, unbuttoning his fly, letting loose an erect penis. Walking over to the stall of the nearest Percheron mare. Reaching up and stroking the mare's withers. Climbing up on the stall gate. Grasping her firmly by the tail, lifting the tail.

Perdue ran around the barn. He pushed closed the barn door Sir had opened. Dropped the heavy bar quietly into place. Ran around to the back of the barn again, where hay had spilled out of the door high in the loft, forming a large pile on the earth. Perdue kicked it all along the wall of the barn. He pulled the fire kit—the flint and striking stone Sir and Gal Sal had given him for Christmas—out of his pants pocket.

Perdue looked once again through the knot-hole. Sir was still hunched over the mare, engaged in an act he had often enough performed more privately. Perdue felt sorry about the animals. Sorry to lose his favourite look-out. He struck the flint to the stone.

There had been no rain on the estate since the crops had needed it, months ago. The hay, then the bone-dry pine of the barn, went up in a flash. Perdue staggered back from the power of the blaze. The fire surged along the wall, up, leaping into the loft. There, the loose piles of hay exploded into flame with a dull *thuuump!*

Above the crackling roar of the fire, Perdue heard the horses screaming, hooves smashing their stalls to pieces. The burning hay, eating rapidly through the floor boards of the loft, dropped down upon the animals, upon Sir. Then the roof around the lantern burst open, sending particles of fire drifting in a high spiral into the clear morning air.

They fell all around the yard, sliding off the sloping copper-sheeted roof of the new stone house, but sticking to and setting alight the roof of the old house. Soon it too burned strongly.

Perdue, dodging the falling rain of fire, ran back into the new house. The girl stood already at the front window. And they stayed there until the barn and the old house had both collapsed in upon themselves, and all that remained were two large mounds of embers, glowing dully in the long twilight of the late autumn.

GEOFFREY URSELL

CHAPTER TWENTY-THREE

THE HOUSE FLOATED upon a white sea. The sea deepened as the snow fell steadily, drifting down in a thick mist of flakes. The snow was a growing tide of purity washing over the black ash of earth.

They had been watching it fall since daybreak, slowly covering all trace of what had passed. The house was warm, a cosy ark floating on the cold sea.

Now, after supper, they sat on the floor, playing a game with the finger bones of the Giant. They each placed a bone in front of them. Then they took turns adding bones on each side of the first bone, turning them slightly towards the other person. They kept doing this, taking turns, and looking closely at the precise positioning of the bones.

Until, when they put down the last of the twenty-four pieces of bone, the circle reaching between them was perfectly complete.

PART

2

CHAPTER ONE

SHE PAUSED at the bottom of the cellar stairs, letting Perdue walk ahead, carrying a glowing lantern. At her back, the row of windows on the west wall formed a sequence of pale square pools of light. In the afternoon, they would let an ever-lengthening wedge of brilliant sun slide across the smooth stone floor. Now the huge space was dim, although she did not need the lantern to see.

She put the last piece of bread and honey from breakfast into her mouth. Her mouth filled with a sharp sweetness. She chewed slowly, then swallowed.

She did not know what Perdue had come to find. He stopped by the brimming well in the centre of the floor. She walked over to the well, bending her head down and dipping her hand into the chill water. She cupped the icy liquid to her lips, swirled it around her teeth, gulped, and traced the sensation of cold as it slid down into her belly.

Perdue watched her drink, then looked around. She followed his gaze as it passed over the walls of the storage rooms, stacked with tins of food, on the east wall, over the walls of the coal bins to the north. He glanced at the door set in the west wall, opening on the long tunnel that led to the meat cellar. She did not move, but waited.

Finally, he turned to the south, walking to the door there. He opened the door, left it open, went in. She moved after him, the stones cool on her bare feet.

Inside a room as long as the entire wall of the cellar, the lantern cast a necessary light. Perdue held it up and ahead in one hand, picking up a long pole with a metal hook at one end in the other. The row of windows that could be seen from the outside of the house was shuttered tight. Not a pin-hole of the morning light striking full force on the other side came through.

Setting the lantern on top of a row of covered bins, with both hands Perdue used the hook at the end of the pole to open shutter clasps and swing the shutters wide. A shaft of sunlight surged in. Millions of motes of dust swam in and out of the light. She blinked her eyes, narrowing them against the glare. The strong sun poured in, soon making the flame in the lamp invisible, a ghost of a flame.

The light fell upon a line of massive bins side by side against the long wall farthest from the windows. It revealed hundreds of large bins along the stone cellar wall itself. And thousands of small bins, really drawers, stacked in tiers on the short walls of the room. All of the bins, the walls, even the floor, were covered with a silvery metal that, struck by the intense sun, dazzled and glinted and bounced the light from glistening surface to surface, filling the room with an overwhelming scintillation of light.

She held her hands up to her eyes, squinted through the

cracks between her fingers. Watched Perdue set the pole down and begin to lift the covers of the bins, to pull open all the drawers.

All of them brimmed with seeds, all sizes and colours of seeds. Seeds for grain, for vegetables, for herbs, for flowers. She was astonished at the treasure of seeds, the glowing mounds of seeds heaped in marvellous plenty. Food they could have been eating all winter. Food they could eat in the winters to come.

Her eyes still narrowed against the light, she went to stand by Perdue. He lifted a handful of seeds and let them trickle back into the bin. The underside of the covers of the bins had square white labels, with varying black script, on them.

"Wheat," Perdue read. "Oats. Barley. Rye." He moved from bin to bin, she beside him. "Celery. Tomatoes. Turnips. Acorn squash, hubbard squash, butternut squash, marrow."

Perdue caressed the seeds, as if trying to feel some force lurking in them. Seeds of petunias and cosmos, nasturtiums and marigolds. Clover seeds, pumpkin seeds, hollyhock seeds. The thick yellow-white seeds of corn, the tiny gold-dark seeds of mustard. Seeds of carrots, Nantes and Chantenay, nearly as small. Grey-black seeds of poppies. Radish seeds.

Cabbage and verbena seeds. Peas and beans. Wax, brittle, broad, lima, snap and scarlet runner beans. Beet seeds and chard seeds. Broccoli and aubergine. Leeks, parsnips, spinach, peppers. Baby's breath and peonies. Leaf, head, and butter lettuce. Bleeding heart and salvia. Stock, primrose, portulaca, lupin, and gloxinia. Seeds of citrons, asters, lilies, columbines. Cucumbers. Coral bells. Shasta daisies. Brussels sprouts. Geraniums, chrysanthemums, clematis and delphiniums. Celosia, calendula, cornflower, strawflower, sunflower, sweet peas!

Bulbs! Of spanish onions, sweet onions, red onions,

silverskins. Bulbs of tulips, gladioli, bulbs of daffodils in seven bins.

Two lines of drawers with aromatic seeds of herbs. Sweet basil and coriander. Parsley, savoury, thyme. Rosemary. Tarragon. Dill, fennel, lavender. Caraway and borage. Marjoram and chives. Horse-radish, horehound, mint, sage, anise.

The room swam with aromas she had never known before.

Perdue opened more drawers, lifting up more seeds of flowers. Begonias, dahlias, zinnias. Carnations and Canterbury bells. Forget-me-nots and everlastings. Sweet-williams.

Morning glories.

Mushroom spawn.

Bins and bins of countless seeds glowing in the brilliant light.

The odour of seeds that had suddenly felt the touch of sun and started to wake from dreams of earth, of rain. The touch of seeds that flowed through hands that soon would lift and carry, carefully plant and tend them. The innumerable caresses of seeds, seeds, seeds. The voices of seeds that suddenly knew how the world, in its ellipse, had finally turned its tilted back around once more to sun, and how the lengthening days spread light and warmth upon the land, and how the melting snow trickled into stirring soil. And the seeds—so still and sleeping through all the cold and dark—the seeds knew, the seeds cried out to be taken from their refuge.

And she knew that Perdue heard something she did not hear, and that he would do now whatever the seeds desired.

CHAPTER TWO

STANDING ON earth moist and warm to her touch, she felt the darkness breathe on her body. Above, the new moon and the stars filled the cool air with glimmering light. She watched Perdue stride in a slow circling way out from the edge of a wide, clear space around the house, the centre. Dipping into the sack at his side, he threw out handfuls of seed, arcs of seed glistening white as they fell to the black earth.

This was her world, the one she knew from the time with her parents, shut out from the world of the sun and the settlers swarming over the land. Sheltering in caves, sleeping all day, and at night coming out to forage and hunt. The darkness their friend.

She knew the shapes, the smells, the sounds of the night. The rustling of bats in the sky and of snakes on the ground. The odour of skunks as they prowled, the whistle of weasels, the sharp bark of raccoons. The swift silence of hunting, the flurry of sound at the kill.

She looked past Perdue and the falling shower of seeds to the town. There the shacks of newcomers had been built on this side of the tracks, and a murmur of sound rose faintly. And there, and beyond, in the centre of town, the lights in the houses, the lights at the corners of streets, flared in the dark like stars that had fallen to earth.

CHAPTER THREE

SHE STOOD on top of the house with Perdue. Stood on the flat, copper-sheathed look-out with the ornamental railing all around and the lightning rod in one corner.

Looking out to the west, Perdue held the binoculars to his eyes. Then he held them out to her. Lifting them up, she looked across the prairie. The land was too bright. She was not used to so much light. She saw a thin dark line, running directly towards her from the far blue horizon of mountains that cut the glowing land in half. The line widened as it got nearer, and she saw the pulsating shapes of wagons rolling on it, driving in and out of town. At a couple of widely separated spaces along the road, tall, square wooden towers had been constructed. They were all a blaze of red, except for the shining, large white letters on them. Seven of the towers stood alongside a railway siding just outside the far end of town. Wagons came to them full of grain and left empty.

She moved the glasses down towards the centre of town, adjusted the focus as Perdue had taught her, and brought into sharper definition the massive rear façade of the completed Government Building.

Behind the high windows, she could see the blurred forms of people—diminished by distance to the size of fingernails even through the binoculars—bustling from room to room, or bent over desks. She tilted the binoculars down slightly more and studied the grounds—trees only somewhat taller than men, hedges, luxuriant flower-beds full of dazzling colours, and spreading, bright-green lawns where long rows of sprinklers spewed gleaming plumes of water.

She dipped her chin a bit more, changed the focus again. Saw line after line of boxcars and flatcars, the colourless shacks of the shanty town crowding up to the tracks. She took the binoculars away from her eyes. Blinked. The Government Building, the grain storage buildings, the railway yards, the shacks, had leapt back into the distance, the nearest structure more than two miles away.

There was no longer a railway track close by, in front of where the old house used to stand. The almost-encircling ridge of buffalo bone had disappeared too, carted off during the winter. Sheltering inside the new stone house, never going out at all, they had not known these things had been done.

Perdue was looking towards the east now, and she turned around too, facing the rising sun, which had not yet lifted out of the clutch of the hills. She sheltered her eyes from the light with her hands. The hills too had changed, had a road that followed all the way around their base, and led off at intervals into the ravines. There were no more sod huts, but many widely set apart farmsteads with white wooden houses and red barns and outbuildings. Grazing cattle, cultivated fields, and gardens.

Gardens. She followed Perdue as he moved to the copper railing and looked down at their garden.

Far from the house, perhaps half a mile or more, the garden began. A trail of plants spiralling slowly, slowly in. All of the plants were mixed together, a few tender stalks of corn with sweet-pea tendrils beginning to twine around them, next to nodding green fronds of young wheat and the tiny feathery plumes of carrots. The first double leaves of peas and beans were breaking through the soil, interspersed with taller shoots of iris and daffodils almost ready to flower. The small fluted leaves of lettuce trembled in the midst of spiky leaves on short vines of cucumber and squash.

It was a path of new green life leading the sun in a closing circle towards the house. Leading the sun in past a froth of leaves on clumps of raspberry bushes and strawberry vines. Leading the sun in towards the grave of the Giant: the true centre, the true heart of this whirling galaxy of plants.

The garden came to a stop at the edge of an inner circle of space that enclosed the ashes of the old house and barn and the new house. And in this space, the wild prairie grasses and the prairie flowers reclaimed the burnt earth, the earth pounded down by the harvest.

Crocuses burst through the soil, and buds of prairie lilies. The tangled roots of long grasses sent shoots surging once more up to the surface. Pale, pale leaves and shoots, which would soon fashion stems and flowers. Yarrow and sweet clover, larkspur and blue-eyed grass. To blanket the charred earth. The ashes of dead bodies helping this life to reassert itself.

And close around the grave of the Giant, their first leaves pushing out from dark-red, thorny stalks, was a circle of rose bushes. Roses Gal Sal planted before she left. Roses soon to bloom to lean their fragrant, nodding heads in over the massive stone.

GEOFFREY URSELL

CHAPTER FOUR

THE SOUND OF rain. The steady small drum, drum, drum on the roof, the swishing flow through the eavestroughs, into the gutters. The mutter of thunder.

She sat on the buffalo robe in her room, looking at rain streaking the window.

Heard the welcome sound of rain. The voiceless celebration of plants. The thunder.

She listened.

The sound of something else. Intermittent. Then more and more steady. A growling roar deeper than the sound of thunder. And whump. Whump. Whump. Steadily louder and louder. WHUMP. WHUMP. WHUMP.

She stood up, went down the hall. Perdue, in his room, breathed calmly, full of sleep.

The low persistent roar came from the west. WHUMP! WHUMP! WHUMP! now came ceaselessly from the east.

She looked towards the end of one of the long halls that crossed where the staircase emerged from below. Through the window there she could see flashes of fire all along the horizon of the hills. Fire that grew solidly into a curtain of flickering red hanging below a layer of black, thick cloud.

The roaring. The steady distant WHUMP! WHUMP! WHUMP! And then the sun, its burning disc slowly sliding up behind the curtain of flame, and the flame fading, paler, paler. The sun rising, pushing into the watery space between earth and cloud. The flame pale, wavering, almost dying out. The sun rising. Moving behind the cloud. Gone. Leaving the red curtain of flame. WHUMP!!! WHUMP!!! WHUMP!!! The grumbling bass roar going on and on. The sun gone. But still the rain. The rain.

The curtain of flame gone.

The roar silenced.

The sound of rain.

Out of the murk at the base of the hills, she thought she saw a darker line move. She walked back into Perdue's room and got the binoculars from where they rested on a window-sill. By the time she returned to the window, she could see clearly that there was not just a line, but what seemed to be a crawling mass coming across the plain from the hills.

She looked through the glasses.

At men on horses in the lead. Men with metal helmets, in dull grey uniforms and rain cloaks. Men carrying long, curved blades and poles with sharp metal points at the end. Horses plodding across the wet earth, churning it into mud.

Behind the horses, men on foot. Thousands and thousands of men. In uniforms. In columns. Slogging through the mud. Carrying guns.

She went to the west window. Looked towards the town. In the railway yards around the station, men in dull brown uniforms were getting out of trains. Thousands and thousands of men. Carrying guns.

Beyond the railway yards, in the park around the Government Building, were hundreds of tents. And stretching out along the shore of the ornamental lake, and farther north along the other side of the river, giant metal tubes pointed at an angle towards the east. The tubes were placed only a stone's throw apart and were banked up in front with walls of sandbags. Their voices were silent now, for the moment.

The columns of men in brown uniforms began marching towards her. She went back to the east window. Those men in grey were much nearer now. It appeared as though the house would be the precise mid-point of their confrontation.

She looked into Perdue's room. He was still sleeping. The pouch that held the Giant's finger bones hung from his waist. Inside the bag, the bones clicked faintly together. She sat down beside Perdue and untied the pouch. She took the bones out, tossed them into the air. The bones fell down into the places they would have been if they had still sheltered inside flesh, held by sinew. She gathered up the bones and put them back.

Into the hall came a faint and trembling light. She got up and went out. Light fell upon the west window like rain. She went to the window and looked down at the source of light. The stone over the Giant's grave throbbed with a luminous force. Pulsations of pale light, veined with brighter tendrils, pushed out from the stone. They formed a glowing hemisphere, a small dome that quickly grew larger and larger, reaching up and out to cover the prairie around the grave, then the house, then the encircling garden. Soon the pale aura reached the edge of the garden, and stopped, almost invisibly in place.

She turned back to the east window. The men on horses had forced their mounts into a gallop. In a long, wavering line that spread out all across the plain, they charged.

They lowered their lances, held their sabres forward at the end of stiff arms. They were not far from the rim of the garden.

She watched them charge. Watched them, as they reached the garden, the faintly glowing dome of light, slide apart in the centre like a herd of buffalo around a massive boulder. Not one of the plants, now much larger and greener, was trampled; not one blossom of a flower was touched.

Behind the charge, the mass of armed men was running now, rank upon rank of men lurching and slipping in the mud. They reached the rim of the garden. Slid around it without breaking step, without stumbling as they swung past.

She turned and walked down the hall to the other end. Before she got there, she could hear a rattling sound, as of dried seeds in a gourd shaken hard. The rattling sound went on and on.

Near the western rim of the garden, half a mile away, the men in brown had strung out a line of guns with large, round barrels. She saw the horses, no longer running, but plunging into the wet earth, kicking useless legs in the air; their riders pitched off, charging the guns with lances, with the bare steel of sabres. Falling.

The rattling sound went on and on. Soon there were no horses on their feet. No riders. Then she saw the other men running, running, rifles lowered, long knives attached to the rifles. Many of them falling into the mud, writhing, then not moving. Others ran over them. To pitch forward on their faces, not to move. Others ran. Fell.

Some of the men at the large guns fell over. The men in grey could not reach most of the large guns. Where they could, they slashed at the men in brown with their knives.

Then the mass of men in brown behind the line of large guns began to run at the men in grey. They also had rifles with long knives on them. They slashed at the men in grey who had reached the large guns. The rattling sound went on and on. Interspersed with the pop! pop! of rifle fire.

The men in grey ran forward, did or did not reach the large guns, fell down, fell down, fell down, until the mound of bodies in front of the large guns grew so large that those behind had trouble climbing over. The mound of bodies reached from one side of the plain to the other. Miles and miles of mounded bodies.

At last the men in grey stopped trying to climb over the mound of bodies. They turned back. Ran past the house again, swirling around the circle of the garden: water around rock.

While they had been confronting the guns, other men had attacked the earth with shovels. The men running back plunged into the trenches that had been made ready for them. Disappeared from the surface of the earth. She knew they were there, but all she could see were clods of mud flung into the air as the trenches went deeper, as new trenches, running back from the front in a zigzag line, were dug.

The men in brown, she saw, on the other side of the line of mounded bodies, were also digging in.

Then, once again, the cannons spoke. And cannons replied from the hills. A strange, whistling screaming filled her ears. Then the shells exploded in mud. Pushing back into the trenches the mud the men had flung from them. Blowing apart the mound of bodies. WHUMP!!! WHUMP!!! WHUMP!!! WHUMP!!! WHUMP!!! WHUMP!!! WHUMP!!! WHUMP!!! on and on.

And never once landing in the spiralling garden, sheltering in the faint luminescence. Never amidst the plants dizzy with rain, the rain surging into their green bodies, the plants trembling and swaying in this most intimate communion. Cells bursting apart with joy. Drinking in the rain, the rain, the rain, the rain!!

CHAPTER FIVE

$\begin{array}{c}\end{array}$ T HE RAIN and the barrage of shells stopped at the same instant.

With spoonfuls of buffalo stew half-way to their mouths, she and Perdue paused, turned to the kitchen window. They put their spoons down and went to the kitchen door. Opened it and stepped outside.

The rays of the high sun, sweeping the clouds apart, filled the plain with radiant light. The wild grass around the house was new-minted gold and green, the blossoms of wild flowers cupping pure water. Around the Giant's stone, the rose bushes were thick with dark, gleaming leaves and with unopened buds. The plants in the garden sighed as they sucked in the glistening droplets clinging to them, as their roots pulsated with the sweet fluid that suffused the earth.

Surrounding the garden was another kind of man-made landscape.

The men in brown and the men in grey had not ceased their activity while the rain fell. They had sent out patrols, forays, expeditions into the space between the trenches. Upon ground ploughed and harrowed by the explosions of thousands of shells, they had laid row upon row of wire with long, sharp barbs, and planted thousands of white wooden crosses on shallow graves.

Yet there were many wounded and dying men who were not underground. They hung upon the strands of wire, lay twisted in the mud, floated in the water of massive holes the shells had gouged out in the earth. Some of the men cried out for help, screamed unceasingly, moaned and moaned, until new bullets struck them, stopped their mouths with lead and the heart's blood.

Into the sky, now perfectly clear above the battlefield, cylindrical shapes rose and hovered. Their coverings were the colour of the men's uniforms, and men in uniform rode in baskets dangling down beneath them. These men pointed at the trenches, at the railway yards, at the distant hills, and sent small packages plummeting to the ground where other men picked them up and ran with them into the trenches.

She and Perdue heard a faint droning noise, as of a swarm of bees very near and coming nearer. But all the bees they could see were happily grappling with the blossoms of flowers. Then, out of the clouds that had moved back in a circle only as far as the half-ring of hills, came large birds—no, not birds—with motionless double wings, but flying faster and higher than birds.

The men on the ground below the floating shapes tried to pull them down. But the flying machines were too swift, diving at them, and the floating shapes burst into flame, and, pouring dark smoke, plunged out of the sky.

Then the flying machines buzzed and twisted, searching out each other. The sun glinted off their brightly coloured wings. They climbed and climbed, losing themselves in the sun, then, plummeting like stones through the air, they pounced, guns chattering. And one by one they were struck, set on fire, fell and smashed into explosion, into extinction.

And while they were flying, fighting each other, down on the ground new metal shapes emerged from the hills and from the trains. Machines that rolled over trenches, clawing their way through the wire, smashing down crosses, crushing down men in the mud. Growling machines with rattling guns firing through slits in the metal.

Then the voices of the cannons came. WHUMP!!! WHUMP!!! WHUMP!!! And the growling machines burst into fragments. Or got caught in the path of fire that spewed like water from tubes in the trenches, liquid fire that covered the growling machines, the men leaping out, running and burning.

On the edge of the wild prairie, gazing out over the garden, she and Perdue silently watched this astonishing world.

CHAPTER SIX

THE STARS were not falling.

To her, and to Perdue, lying on their backs, cradled by the prairie grasses, it seemed as if they were. They knew the stars were not dropping out of the sky, slamming into the air, bursting apart in dazzling flares of every colour except that of the golden sun.

Yet, over their heads, the night sky exploded with strange light in harsh instants of illumination. Moment upon moment the colour of the sky and earth shifted. Everything was at once icy red, then bleak white, then sallow green.

The men in the trenches could not trust the dark. Out of it might come murderous figures. Death looming up, a clear dark silhouette against the cold, round moon.

CHAPTER SEVEN

THE RISING SUN.

The clear sky.

A breeze drifting east to west.

Amidst leaves beaded with dew, she helped Perdue to gather food from the garden. Damp soil clung to the light orange of new carrots, to small white-brown potatoes. Peas and lettuce were a delicate milky-green. Beans a pale, fuzzy yellow. The tender flesh of plants gently touched fingers, fell into wicker baskets. Around the just-forming ears of corn throbbed the blue and purple and deep crimson of morning glories. The plucked blossoms of sweet peas overflowed one basket, then another. The air was scented with the perfume of plants.

Bees hummed back and forth from the flowers to their hive under the eaves of the house, near where barn swallows were nesting. Robins hopped through the grass. A meadow lark, perched on top of the roof, welcomed the flourishing light.

From out of the long line of quiet trenches towards the hills, a ghostly cloud began to rise. It was not the innocent white of clouds in the sky. It was thick yellow-green, a festering pus of cloud that steadily lifted higher and higher until it became a towering wall. The wall slid across the pulverized slop of earth, hiding the wire, the crosses, the scurrying rats that lunged for their burrows. It slid into shell holes, filled them, and lingered.

They looked up from their work to watch the wall of cloud drift with a breeze that wafted it safely around the rim of the garden, wafted it closer and closer to the other men sheltering in the other line of trenches.

The cloud reached that line. Part of it sank down, seeking a place to rest. The men there smelled the pus smell of the cloud, and most did not have time to keep it out of their lungs. Did not have time to cover their faces with masks. It filled up their lungs.

The cloud was thick. She and Perdue could not see through it. But they heard what it did. At first there were screams. But the air once expelled in a scream had to be replaced, and the cloud took its place. And then the choking began, the gasping for air that was clean.

The cloud moved on, drifting towards the railway yards, the town. But the breeze lifted it, began to scatter its force.

Yet the men in the trenches had been gripped by its power. They crawled up from the shelter of the earth, vomiting, coughing. Their faces were no longer the colour of flesh, but the colour of the cloud. Yellowish-green turning blue turning grey, ashy grey. And their mouths slobbered froth, green froth.

The breeze shifted and started drifting back from west to east. And now from the trenches where the men had been crawling forth issued a new cloud, a cloud of mustard yellow, dense, heavy, sliding at the other line of trenches. Sinking down into them. And the other men screamed, leapt from their refuge. Huge blisters rose from their flesh and burst open, fluid pouring out.

The men closest to the garden seemed, in their throes of agony, to see the garden now. They crawled, they staggered towards it. They reached the edge. Their flesh was ghastly green, was a mass of open wounds. Their bulging eyes stared and stared.

They saw. They wanted to enter. They saw the garden, the house. They saw the naked girl and boy, the naked children, standing there, baskets of vegetables, of flowers on their arms, at their feet. They wanted to be in the garden. But they could not enter.

They lay down in the mud where no plant lived. Now that the poison clouds had passed, the rats once more appeared. The men were not yet dead. They flailed the rats away. Their hands reached out, they implored.

She did not know if she could save any of them. The men reached out to her, as her father had reached out, trying to pull death out of his body. She had not been able to help her father. Now she took a step towards the garden's edge. She stepped outside the circle's charm.

The stench hurled itself upon her, smashed into her body. The stench of exploding shells, of the lingering poison of the clouds, of the bloated meat of horses, of the rotting slop of bodies that had been men. The stench hammered her down to her knees.

She dropped the basket. The flowers withered, turned brown and dry. The vegetables melted to black slime.

She felt the chill ooze suck at her flesh. She looked into the staring eyes of men turning into corpses. She opened her mouth wide, her belly heaving up what she needed to build her own life, to grow. She got to her feet. Bullets zipped, zipped, zipped around her. The men reached their hands out to her. She staggered backwards, fell half inside

GEOFFREY URSELL

112

the garden, crushing plants beneath her.

Perdue pulled her entirely inside.

The smell of the garden, the smell of the prairie, the hum of bees, the songs of birds flowed into her.

Overhead, the real clouds had gathered. Clouds dark and ponderous with rain. It started to rain. The drops fell slowly, splashing into her face, washing the vomit away from her mouth, washing her eyes clean of what they had seen. She breathed the sweet smell of the rain deep into her lungs.

The rain washed over the men now dead in the mud. The rats ate the dead flesh. The rain fell more steadily, turning into a downpour. Touching the ravaged bodies, the rain began to soften them, and the bodies started to dissolve. The flesh melted in the rain, melted away out of the mouths of the rats. The flesh washed away from the skulls, from the bones. The rain fell with more and more force. The skulls began to melt in the rain. The bones liquefied, oozed into fluid earth.

The rain dissolved the barbed wire, the crosses. Mud flowed into the shell holes, into the trenches, levelling them. The rain thickened, poured down in a flood. She felt as if she were at the bottom of a river where she could still somehow breathe.

The rain hid the violent world.

The rain washed it away.

CHAPTER EIGHT

SHE HAD NEVER been here before. She stood in front of the door, at the end of the stone tunnel connecting this place with the cellar. She put the lantern on the floor to one side. With both hands she pulled down the long, metal handle and swung the massive door open. A wintry chill flowed out, enveloping her.

She picked up the lantern, stepped inside, put the lantern down again, and pulled the door shut. She heard the heavy latch click into place.

She left the lantern, gleaming palely, by the door. She went further in. Her feet sank into a thick, spongy layer of sawdust. The air was completely motionless, freezing cold. Her expelled breath turned to puffs of white mist. She saw that blocks of ice were piled on both sides of the corridor she moved along and were carved into a high arc overhead.

She reached another corridor that intersected at right

angles with this central one. There seemed to be nothing there. She moved on, the light from the lantern fading into a glimmering sheen upon the ice. Past several more intersecting corridors. All empty.

Over her head, she knew, was a great thickness of earth. And on the surface of that earth grew the prairie.

The cold seeped into her, but she did not shiver. She knew there was something important here. Something for her to find. She moved on. Reached the next corridor.

Looking along it, saw pale things hanging. She entered the corridor, went closer. Her eyes, so used to the night, saw clearly.

The long, long row of bodies. Cut in halves. Suspended from beams. Hung on large metal hooks. Their glistening shapes mottled pale red and white. Bodies fading into the farther darkness.

She went to another corridor. More bodies. And another. More. She walked into the dark, the lantern only a small gleaming star far behind.

She felt a sound rising in her chest, pushing at her throat. She stood, surrounded by the bodies, her hands touching the icy flesh. The sound pushed out through her mouth, shaping her tongue, her lips. Making itself into a high-pitched, wavering cry. A keening that rose and fell. A sound she had heard her mother sing as they stood at night on the rim of the river valley looking down at the place the tribe had been destroyed by the river of blood.

She closed her eyes. And singing, her heart spoke its longing. Singing, she saw the vast prairie covered with living buffalo. Saw the incredible, endless herds. Felt the heat of midsummer upon her. Heard the marvellous sound of grazing, millions of mouths ripping grass, munching. The thundering, guttural roars of countless bulls in rut, throwing themselves down in dust wallows, the dust rising thick in the hot, swirling air. Calves lowing, calves suckling.

She stood on the great rock shaped like a buffalo sitting

down and looked out over the prairie. She saw the hunters on horseback approaching, the buffalo running begin, the buffalo stampeding, leaving a trail of fallen beasts with arrows in their hearts. The women skinning off the hides, cutting up the meat, eating raw morsels still hot, piling the cut meat onto the hides. The hunters, returning, joining the first feast of brains and warm blood.

And singing, she slid down off the rock to join them, and found herself chilled to the bone, alone in the bitter dark.

CHAPTER NINE

IT WAS WARM on the Giant's stone.
She and Perdue lay upon it, turned on their sides to face one another, shelling and eating peas from the basket between them. The peas were crisp, with a sweet juice that left a slight tartness tingling in her mouth.

The light of the sun danced through drifting white clouds. A small breeze stirred, wafting a wonderful fragrance.

Around them, the bushes were heavy with blooms, astonishing roses filling the air with a dense honey smell. Velvety petals of deepest blood-red, petals of pink, petals pure white. Huge blossoms dripping with scent.

And, mingled with this, the fragrance, strange and keen, of the prairie around, its wild grasses swaying, its wild flowers surging up to the sun.

And more: the smells of the garden. A garden amazingly

grown, now lush and luxuriant. The garden plants rejoicing in the perfect conditions for growth, thriving beyond their own dreams. Racing to vegetable fullness, exploding in masses of flowers.

The garden grew, hiding the town and the hills beyond from their sight. It rose up, enclosing and sheltering them.

CHAPTER TEN

SHE HEARD the sound of some creature pushing its way through the garden long before she saw any sign of what it was. She also heard a voice, a gruff, squeaking voice that sounded angry, full of spite.

Perdue, she knew, was somewhere in the garden.

She stayed on the Giant's stone, hidden behind the rose bushes, peeking out.

She saw a black, shiny cylinder bobbing up and down through the mass of plants. The shiny cylinder approached. Under it appeared the large and bony face of a man. He thrashed clear of the garden. He wore a black cloth jacket that had long tails of cloth hanging down at the back, a creamy white shirt with a black bow tied over the throat, a pleated cloth of red silk around his waist, dark-grey trousers with thin, paler-grey stripes, and gleaming black shoes. The clothes had been cut to fit his shrunken body, his squat and bowed legs perfectly. In one gloved hand he carried a golden cane; in the other a thin, small white tube that smoked at one end.

He stopped, looked around.

"Those fools," he said, "of course it's still here. Burned down, they said. Nothing but wheat fields. What's all this then? Garden. Big house. Rose bushes."

He moved towards the roses. As he approached, she could see that the skin of his face had a slight golden sheen, as if it were partly made of that metal. He saw her eyes looking out at him.

"And what do we have here?" He parted the bushes with one white-gloved hand. "Come out my dear," he waved her forward. "Let's have a look at you."

She stepped out into the open. The man made her slowly spin around with nudges of his golden cane. She felt the icy touch of the tip of his cane on her thigh, her buttock. He stopped turning her.

"Yes," he said. "Yes. Very nice."

He slid the cane towards where her legs joined. "But not ready yet."

And then Perdue was beside him, striking the cane down. With a sudden whirling motion, the dwarf slipped a gleaming blade from inside the cane and whipped it across Perdue's belly. A thin red line welled up, blood leaping out of the long wound, trickling in brilliant beads down the brown skin. Perdue did not flinch. He flicked out a foot, kicking the blade out of the dwarf's hand. It flew over her head, smashing onto the Giant's stone, shattering.

"Ah," the dwarf said, facing Perdue and bowing, "it's you. My apologies. Is your father inside?" He motioned towards the house. He glanced at the house, at the curtainless windows. "I suppose not. Too bad. I had a business proposition for him. New forces at work now. All this," he announced, waving the burning tube from side to side, "will have to go."

He laughed. The smell of the burning tube was bitter. She coughed.

"There's a new plan." He began to speak louder. "We must ensure the material conditions of prosperity! And how? Machinery! Machinery."

He stopped. "I'd advise you to get out," he said. "Get out while you can."

He turned his gaze back upon her. "I'll always have a place for her," he told Perdue. "I'll come back for her later." He put the white tube in his mouth, drawing his breath in so that the end turned glowing red.

"But just remember," he continued, releasing smoke from his mouth, from his nose as he talked, "you don't have long. The new forces can't be stopped. Machines can't be stopped."

Smiling, he walked away from them, entered the garden, thrashing his way through the plants. Soon only the black cylinder of his hat could be seen floating unsteadily above the foliage, the flowers. Then he was gone.

She moved to Perdue. The blood from the wound had thickened, had stopped trickling down his belly. She put a hand on his chest, looked into his eyes. She saw the hurt in them. He put his hand over hers, held it. His face was pale, his body trembling.

She helped him to lie down, then went into the house for water to cleanse the wound. The plants she would need to cover it grew in the prairie around.

CHAPTER ELEVEN

THEY HEARD the scream of whistles even as they lost sight of the dwarf. So, after she had dressed his wound, they went to the roof of the house.

There, she watched with Perdue as train after train, pulling hundreds of flatcars piled high with long metal bars, rolled into town. A throng of men from the shanty town gathered to watch and were soon at work.

They graded earth, levelled gravel, and laid track for a spur line leading from the rail yards towards the ornamental lake. One of the trains backed down the spur line, and gangs of men unloaded the metal bars. Others carried load after load of earth on barges out into the middle of the lake and dumped it into the water.

Working in the opposite direction, another throng of men, using teams of horses, dragged ploughs on a line straight through the tall, green crops directly towards the hills. They heaped the earth into a long ridge, and, with huge round weights pulled by horses, shaped it and rolled it into a road. Halfway to the hills, a crossing road going north and south was started. Soon the roads reached the hills, sending offshoots to all the farms there. Along the lengths of the roads, tall poles were set up and strung with wires.

To the west, beyond the bridge that had now been constructed across the lake—with room for a train on the first level and a roadway above—men continued to lay tracks through the town and then alongside the road that already cut the distant prairie in half. It was clear that it would not take them long to reach the mountains far away.

To the south, another train unloaded machines that began to eat into the base of the hills. Several buildings were set up, and smoke began rising from them.

More trains brought in machines of glistening coloured metal and glass. People got into the machines and drove them up and down the roads, plumes of dust rising into the air behind their shapes. Some of these machines had open boxes at their backs, and these, going into the hills, returned with loads of men from the farms, who laughed and shouted with pleasure at the new sensation of speed.

The machines carried them over the bridge and into the centre of town. There, they clambered over the old wooden buildings, ripping them apart, knocking them into rubble. In their places they raised skeletons of metal bars, fastening them together with clanging sounds and with showers of flame. The men scrambled everywhere upon the metal, lifting new beams high into place, then walking across them. Several times men fell, small fluttering shapes that made no sound.

Around some of these metal skeletons, the men built

walls of the reddish-brown brick that came back on the train from the south. Around the larger skeletons, they built walls of stone, carried back by the trains now returning from the mountains. The stone walls, not the creamy-white stone of the Government Building or their home, rose tall and slate-grey into the bright midsummer sky.

All day, men had also been working on the dome of the Government Building, fastening gold leaf all over it. Now it was transformed, a dazzling beacon that would be visible for at least fifty miles on clear days such as this. It had become a small sun, floating over the new buildings of the town below.

At the very top of the dome, a group of men were hauling up something shrouded in canvas, sliding it up the arc of the dome. It reached the top, and they secured it in place on the roof of the cupola. A long rope trailed down to the ground.

There, a crowd of people gathered, the men dressed just as the dwarf was dressed, the women in bright, long dresses, carrying pastel-coloured parasols. Men in red uniforms stood in a line. From the centre of town, a machine that gleamed deep purple and gold rolled across the bridge. The crowd cheered when they saw the machine approaching. It stopped in front of them. Out of it climbed the dwarf. The echoes of his voice, made somehow enormously loud, reverberated faintly in the air.

She and Perdue heard, "Progress . . . prosperity . . . commerce . . . destiny!" Then the distant noise of the crowd cheering wildly.

The dwarf grasped the rope that dangled from the dome. He pulled. The shroud of canvas on top of the cupola hung slack in the still air. Then it trembled and began to slide apart. Then fell away entirely, fluttering down the surface of the dome to the earth far below.

A figure of gold stood revealed. Above gleaming outspread wings that sprouted from its back, the figure lifted

GEOFFREY URSELL

124

outstretched arms that held aloft in each hand a golden torch.

That evening, looking towards the new horizon of tall, solid shapes that thrust up at the setting sun, she listened with Perdue to the wild cries of celebration turn to anger and fighting. Then shots.

In the morning, they watched a mass of men straggling back down the road. The waiting hills gathered them in without a sound.

CHAPTER TWELVE

THE SUN WAS fierce, high over-head. The air was dry. There was not enough wind to move clouds.

She sat with Perdue in the small patch of shade on the north side of the house, their backs resting against cool stones.

To their ears came a faint rustling. The sound grew, became louder, more agitated. It seemed to come from no particular direction, to come from all around.

They stood up, listening.

The sound grew louder still, until it surrounded them. It was coming from everywhere beyond the garden. They walked across the strip of prairie, eased their way through the burgeoning plants. They reached the rim of the garden, and looked out on green fields of grain, still in the heat, only the waves of heat rippling upon the green sea. No wind at all.

GEOFFREY URSELL

Yet the sound, louder now, filled the air. Seemed to rise up from the earth itself. So they looked down.

And saw the earth simmering with movement, the soil all but hidden from sight. The bodies of tiny green creatures were covering the land, climbing the stalks of wheat. Trying to reach the tender, young kernels.

The land was a seething mass of insects. The fields of wheat now were trembling, beginning to sway as if blown by the wind. The rustling sound grew louder and louder. The sun was still beating down.

The grain began to sway and fall as if cut by invisible scythes. The sound of innumerable jaws eating the juicy grain, the flesh of plants, became a clicking, gurgling roar.

The sea of grain was consumed, vanished.

In its place was a sea of grasshoppers. Those that had eaten the grain were now themselves devoured by those who came later. Jaws snapped bodies apart to get at the chewed pulp inside.

The earth boiled with grasshopper bodies.

Then the wind came.

Hot gusts at first, lifting swirls of grasshoppers briefly into the air. Then a harder wind. A parched wind. Blowing harshly from the east. Carrying swarms of grasshoppers high, scorching them, dropping them down, with the grasshoppers whirling their wings in pain.

And the hot wind blew. Drying the grasshoppers out. Killing them. Tumbling the husks of dead insects along the ground. And sucking the moisture out of the now naked earth. Splitting the soil into crazed networks of cracks, of deep fissures.

The wind blew. The land turned to dust. The dust soared into the air. The wind began to circle back upon itself. It raced around the limits of the hills. A frenzy of wind. A wind going mad.

The wind spun and spun, racing now in a huge ring. It sucked up the dust, fed on the dust, gave itself shape with the dust.

Gophers, lifted high in the air, dug tunnels as if they were still underground, and a badger, claws scrabbling, dug after them. Barbed-wire fences, with crows fastened to posts by air too thick to fly in, were flung by. Herds of cattle, mooing plaintively, tumbled through a sky that was no longer sky. Barns sailed past, and houses. The wind grew stronger. It lifted up entire hills, whirling them around before setting them down in a new order.

The dust thickened. The spinning shape of the dust soon formed an impenetrable black wall. The raging whirlwind of dust tightened and tightened around the sheltered circle of the garden and prairie and house. The swirling walls of dust reached the rim of the garden. They rose straight up, howling and shrieking.

From the still centre of a vast cone of screaming wind and dust, she and Perdue looked up and up. They tipped their heads as far back as they could. Until at last they saw a small, small circle of blue with a bright, burning core of sun.

CHAPTER THIRTEEN

AT LENGTH, the whirlwind died down. The land reappeared, stripped of life, dry. Great drifts of powdery soil lay along the lines of poles, rising nearly to the wires at their tops. Across the land tumbled multitudes of thistles, large prickly balls that caught upon and formed into great piles against the once high wires.

A long train of boxcars, its whistle hooting mournfully, rolled into town from the west. Men in shabby clothes were jammed into the train. Many of them perched on the roofs or clung to the sides of the boxcars. The train came across the bridge over the dry lake bed and stopped in the middle of the rail yards. The men clambered down. They unfurled a banner and lifted it up on long wooden poles. Cheering, they began to march towards the Government Building.

She and Perdue, watching from the top of the house

through binoculars, saw lines of men in red uniforms and men in dark-blue uniforms form up at the edge of the gardens of the Building. The mass of marching men came to a halt in front of this line. Several of them moved forward to talk with the leader of the men in uniforms.

The leader pointed back towards the train. The marchers argued, shouted. The leader pulled out a gun. He fired into the air, over their heads. All of the marchers surged forward, yelling. Some of the men in red and blue levelled their guns and fired. Many of the marchers fell down. Others, picking up rocks from the rail yards, threw them at the uniformed men.

But they could not face the guns very long. Dropping their banner, they turned and ran back towards the train. Scrambling under it or leaping through the doors of the boxcars, open on both sides, they raced for the shelter of the shanty town. The men in uniform followed them.

Later that day, the train, once more filled to overflowing with the men in shabby clothes, went back the way it had come.

GEOFFREY URSELL

CHAPTER FOURTEEN

FROM OUT OF the barren hills, from out of the grey and peeling farm buildings, the procession came. As it drew nearer, she and Perdue could see that two figures were at its front.

The first of these was a thin man who wore a dusty, frayed dark suit with a dirty white collar high upon his throat. He had pieces of glass over his eyes, held in place with silver rims. The other had on a long robe, blood-red in colour. His face was hidden behind a white mask, with openings for the eyes and nose. Upon his head was a tall, fantastic hat, a red cone with strange criss-cross markings in black.

Behind these two, a great number of men, women, and children shuffled through the drifting dust. Their clothes were faded and patched. Their faces were lined with dust. They looked hungry, thirsty.

The procession came to a halt at the edge of the garden.

The man in the suit, a much smaller man than the other in the robe, peered towards the garden, his blue eyes sparkling as he appeared to see it. He turned to the people.

"Yes," he said, "I knew it was there. The promised land is before us, ready for us to enter in, if only we will help one another, love one another." His face was fervent, his gestures animated, but he was whispering so quietly that only a very few people, bending their heads close to his mouth, could hear what he was saying.

Others further back called out, "What's he say?"

Those who had heard called back, "He says the promised land is right here! Right in front of our eyes!"

Those who had asked crowded closer, peering ahead. They scoffed, "There's nothing there. Not a goddamn thing but dust!"

The man's glasses flashed in the sun as he raised his eyes towards the dust-dimmed sky. "I know it's there," he whispered. "I can see it. Can't you see it? It's the promised land here on earth, just waiting for us to enter in!"

Those who had heard repeated this information again. And again those who could not see anything but dust laughed bitterly. A few, staring hard, said that they thought they could see something there. Something faint, but something. One or two of the very youngest children walked towards the garden, pointing at it with small, dirty fingers. "Look," they announced. "Look at the flowers."

The man who whispered beckoned to the children. "Out of the mouths of babes," he said. "You must believe. If enough of you believe, then we may all enter in."

Then the other, the one in the white mask, laughed a raucous shriek. His voice was a shrill scream, his words blurred by the mask.

"You are fools to listen to him! He's deceiving you! Telling you lies, poisonous lies!"

Everyone heard him and gathered around to listen,

GEOFFREY URSELL

132

although one or two still stood close to the smaller man, waiting for his next whispered words.

The one behind the mask screamed once more, thrusting his right hand into the air again and again as he spoke. "We must build a new order! A new man! We are on the turning point of an age, and we—you and I together—*we* have the power to shape that new age!! Listen to me!" he screamed. "We must follow the eternal values, the eternal force! We must build for eternity!!"

The crowd began to draw close around him. He went on, his voice rising to a piercing shriek. "This isn't your fault!" He swept his arms wide to take in the dead land. Then he pointed towards the shanty town. "They've done it! Those intruders! They are full of decay, full of filth! They must be eliminated!! Then we can build the new order!!"

The smaller man shook his head. "No," he whispered. "No. That's not true."

But the other went on, his right hand stabbing the air. "Follow me and you will be in touch with God! You will be acting in harmony with Almighty Providence! There is no other way! The new order must come!! But first we must clear away this filth! Clear it away!!"

As if obeying his command, all of the men and most of the women who were not carrying infants began to run, stumbling through the drifts of dust, towards the shanty town. "Clear it away! Away!!" they shouted. The man in the white mask trailed after them, screaming, his blood-red robes flapping in the wind.

The man who whispered looked at the garden again, moved closer, seemed to see her figure and that of Perdue. "The strong must help the weak," he whispered. "If we believe in the brotherhood of man, there is hope. Then the hungry will be fed, the naked clothed, the fallen lifted up." Tears glistened in his eyes.

He looked at them, seemed to look into her eyes. He

whispered, "I know you're there." He reached out his hand. It went through the invisible barrier of pale light. She reached out. She touched his warm, trembling hand.

His eyes widened in joy. He grasped her hand, and stepped into their realm.

He saw them, saw the incredible garden. "You *are* here," he whispered. "You *are*. And this..." he paused, then went on, "*is* Paradise. Thank you," he whispered. "Thank you for letting me see, really see."

On the wind, the screams of "Filth! Filth! Clear it away!" reached them more faintly now. But the man turned to listen when he heard.

"I . . . can't," he said, louder. "I can't stay. Not just myself." Reluctantly, he let go of her hand.

"I must try and help them. Stop them before they do harm." His voice was stronger. "They're good people, really."

He looked around at the garden, a fierce longing in his eyes. "But now I've seen it. It's really here. Now I know! I know!" he shouted, surprising himself.

They heard a thin cry of pain in the distance, saw a mass of shouting figures confronting one another at the edge of the shanty town.

"Thank you," he said again. His voice was clear and strong.

He stepped back, holding them and the garden in his sight. Then suddenly he turned, began to run towards the shanty town, swiftly, lightly, across the barren dust.

"Wait!!" they heard him shout in a commanding tone. "Wait!!! Don't listen to him! We have to work together! Together!!"

CHAPTER FIFTEEN

THE HORN OF the half-moon was flung through the night, flying away above the herd of clouds running below its light. She lay on her back on the long prairie grass, its swaying strands caressing her skin. She held the horn of the moon in her eyes, felt the pull of the moon in her thighs, in her belly below where the soft down of hair now grew. Felt the pull of the moon in her breath, in her new-forming breasts.

The light of the moon swept her, then shadows and dark, like the pulse in her blood, again and again. The blood beating full in her body. The throb of the blood. Her mother had told her that this was to come. At the thought of her mother, her eyes filled with tears.

Inside her belly a drumming began, heavy and deep. She placed her hands there, and under their touch held the gathering force.

Above her the buffalo clouds thundered by, the white ghosts of buffalo racing on high. She saw their eyes flashing, their hooves striking fire.

The drum beating harder. The pulse of this rhythm flowing inside. Her hands sliding down. Touching the warm, the wet rush.

She held up her hand, glistening, dark, to the vanishing moon, blurred by the tears in her eyes.

The stampeding buffalo covered the sky.

GEOFFREY URSELL

CHAPTER SIXTEEN

SHE FELT cool drops of rain on her skin even as the rays of the mid-morning sun, slanting out of a clear blue space of sky, touched her with their warmth. The thunder-shower passed, a small, fluffy cloud, trailing a veil of rain down to earth. A light breeze wafted over her body, stealing the glistening moisture away. Raindrops beaded the prairie grass at her feet; water steamed from the damp soil.

Leaving the open space of prairie, she stepped into the garden, into a world of green shade. The plants arched together high over her head. She shivered. It was much cooler, but she did not shiver because of that. These plants were still so new to her, so strange. And they had flourished so incredibly, as if they were to be food for a race of giants.

From the moist, crumbling earth, labyrinths of roots

drew nourishment up into myriads of leaves. The huge stalks of corn and tree-trunk stems of sunflowers formed a system of support for countless twining plants. Finger-thick vines of peas looped through the air, dangling great pods plump with fruit. Yellow and green beans hung down in thick clusters.

She moved further into the garden, past bright-orange pumpkins that came up to her waist, past large solid cores of cabbages perching at the centre of unfolded leaves that creaked to the touch of her hands. Clumps of enormous spiky leaves, moved aside, revealed massive dark-green glossy orbs and elongated pale-yellow shapes of squash. The crinkled light green of fan-like lettuce leaves glimmered.

She trailed her fingers through the feathery tops of carrots, touched the dusty-green spikes of onions, the leaves like huge green arrowheads—veined with dark red—of beets. She felt the weight of immense globes of tomatoes, of massive purple egg-plants, of giant green and red peppers.

Over all this towered stalks of corn. Cobs as long as her arm pushed away from the stalks, covered in tight leaves and erupting in masses of long, silky hair, pale gold turning to pale red. And she heard the leaves of the corn rustling together high above, whispering the earth's secrets to each other.

And everywhere in that tapestry of plants she saw woven the colours of flowers. Flowers the yellow of the sun, flowers blue and white and pale pink and purple and vivid crimson. Great plumes and feathers of flowers: flowers like exploding balls of colour, flowers like bells. Flowers with thousands of tiny blossoms that sheltered close to the ground. Sunflowers pushing one mighty bloom into the air, dazzling bright-gold petals ringing a profusion of seeds.

The garden was filled with the resonant hum of bees,

GEOFFREY URSELL
138

with the flashing colours and trilling voices of birds, of orange butterflies fluttering, and the iridescent blue bodies of dragon-flies coupling in flight. It was filled with a fragrance compounded of countless odours she had never known before. The scents of flowers, bursting with pollen. The exhalations of vegetables. The aromatic power of herbs: of dill, basil, marjoram, thyme, oregano, summer savoury, suffusing the air.

She tasted the ripeness of raspberries, strawberries crushed in her mouth, their sweet blood swirled by her tongue, trickling into her body.

At last, she stepped back out of the garden, releasing herself from the urgent force of its life.

And stood once more on the prairie. Lost in amazement. Recovering the slow drift of time.

CHAPTER SEVENTEEN

ALL DAY the packs of machines, painted bright red, bright orange, bright green, had ranged over the land: smoothing it, seeding, and spraying.

That night she went out with Perdue into the levelled and empty fields, under the bright half-moon and the stars. When she and her parents had walked out at night, they moved in a land throbbing with life, the air resonant with sound, redolent with scent.

Now there was stillness. No creatures roamed about. They heard no vital sounds. Just, in the distance, the dull roar of the city. The roar of machines running over the land, of other machines rising and falling out of the air.

No pleasant smells. But a lingering trace of something corrupted; a strange, sweet venom rising up from the earth.

The earth itself was not soft below the feet, but hard, as

if turning to rock. And row upon row of thin, sickly leaves just pushing through were tiny, sharp blades slashing at flesh.

The city itself oozed out across the land, leaving a long trail of lights, as slugs leave their slime.

They did not go far, and entered the garden once more with relief.

CHAPTER EIGHTEEN

SHE WATCHED Perdue pull the cork out of another bottle and set it with all the others on the table in the middle of the room. The flame of the lamp was being split into hundreds of miniature flames by the surfaces of bottles. But inside them, the amber, the ruby-red, the coppery, the limpid fluids trembled with the glow from the light.

Perdue moved silently across the spongy cork floor to a shelf. Upon all four sides of the cellar store-room there was row after row of bottles. Tall round bottles set upright, with labels that said "Highland Whisky", "London Gin", "Best Jamaica Rum"; squat bottles shoulder to shoulder labelled "Napoleon Brandy" and the year 1845. Rows of bottles lying down, "Baron de Gervignac, 1883", "Mouton Cabernet, 1887", "Prince d'Alsace, 1872". Thicker bottles, "Champagne de Heidseick, 1894", "Champagne de Roi

Louis XIV, 1891". There were large wooden casks in a row all the way around the bottom of the shelves.

Brushing away cobwebs, Perdue lifted a bottle from its cork-lined shelter. He carried it to the table, took out the cork, put it down on the green-felt surface. The drawer of the table from which he had taken the corkscrew was open. It was also layered with green felt, had hollows in which lay a dozen more corkscrews, long silver spoons, ice tongs, and tiny silver cups. Perdue took out several of the cups. She helped him fill the cups one after the other from various bottles.

They sniffed at the liquids. In some she thought she smelled earth, smelled wood; in others she smelled strange fruits, bitter and sweet. In all she smelled things far away, distant in space and time. Perdue dipped the tip of his tongue into one of the cups. She did the same. Her tongue tingled, felt as if it might be seared, but it was not. She pulled her tongue back inside her mouth. The scent that was locked inside the liquid, released by the heat of her body, instantly flared up, startled her, then faded.

There was something there, some place, some land-scape, some different weather she thought she had dreamed.

She took a sip of the distillation, swirled it around, swal-lowed. Again felt the faint burning, again the sense of something she thought she knew from dreams. Again the fading sensation before knowledge could be grasped, be held and understood.

They began to drink from the cups. She wanted to be able to remember, had to remember. Her throat, her chest grew warm. She poured slow fire into her body.

They filled the cups again. Drank the smoke of wood long burned, the sweet essence of plants long harvested. All held in these bottles and awaiting this release.

The flame in the lamp, the hundreds of miniature flames in the bottles began to shiver, to blur. The outlines of the room shifted. She stepped back from the table. The table swayed. The floor was not as level as it had been. It was difficult to find a solid place to put a foot down. She watched Perdue tip another cup of liquid into his mouth. He seemed very far away.

Her body was hot. The fire of dreamed knowledge was in her, burning faster now, and still she could not understand it. The fire burned higher. Her forehead burned. She wiped sweat away from her eyes. She turned, stumbling out of the room. Without the lamp, she couldn't see the stairs of the cellar clearly. She stumbled back to a wall, and with one hand on the wall, began to walk in a circle until she reached the stairs. She climbed carefully up.

The fire burned further into her now. Burned down into her belly, down into the space that sheltered there. It throbbed, warm and suddenly awake.

A moon nearly full spilled cool light into the hall windows on the ground floor of the house. There was something, something she felt she had to find. She went into a room. It was empty, and the floor shimmered like moving water in the moonlight. She walked across the water into another room. That room was empty too.

She went into room after room. All were empty. There were no chairs and tables, no sideboards in the diningroom, no stuffed chesterfields or armchairs in the drawing-rooms, no billiard-table in the billiard room, no books in the towering empty shelves of the library.

She went back into the hall. The space in her belly was aching now.

The stairs. The stairs swayed. She grasped the banister. Began to climb. The stairs spiralled round and round. Loomed up enormously high. She could scarcely lift her legs high enough. She reached the top.

Down the hall, she knew, was her room. Down the hall. But which hall? There were six, nine, too many. Through several of the windows at the end of the halls to the west, the moon was brightest. Water from the moon came pouring in the windows. It would be cool. Yes, she would immerse herself in that water, would cool her burning body. The fire was good, she liked the fire, but it was getting too hot. Cooler. Just a little cooler.

She put a hand on the walls, felt one wall. Did not look down at her feet. They were too far away. The water. The water from the moon. Must lie down in that water. Cool. Cool. Cool. She headed for the water.

She leaned on the wall. The wall ended too soon. She lurched sideways, falling onto the buffalo robes in her room.

She floated on a pool of moon water. Her long gleaming hair flowed out from around her head, flowed over the small mounds—at their centres dark red nipples—on her chest, flowed over her belly, over the fuzz of hair between her legs, over her thighs, her knees, flowed down to curl and drift at her feet. The moon water, cool and still, rippled around her. The sign of the moon rested on her chest.

She saw Perdue swaying in the doorway. The thing between his legs stuck out hard, straight in front of his body. He moved closer, dipped one foot into the pool of moon water. He touched the thing between his legs with his hand, clasped his hands around it. He moaned.

She floated, a beautiful chill covering her body, beginning to drift into dream.

Perdue swayed, his hands twisting back and forth. She saw a silvery fluid spurt out from him, fall in a brief arc into the pool. And saw Perdue slowly fall, plunging his body too into the cool, cool water of the moon.

CHAPTER NINETEEN

A WAILING SCREAM rose and fell in loudness and pitch, rose and fell. The scream went on and on. Brilliant columns of light leapt up from the earth, piercing the black night. The shafts of light probed the sky, circling, crossing, weaving together, separating, weaving together again. The scream went on and on.

Her head throbbed with pain. Her body ached. Perdue stood beside her. They held hands.

The searching light found, high, high in the dark, hundreds of little silver crosses that glinted when the light struck them. Then the earth began to flare up, red flashes of flame spouting forth. PUM! PUM! PUM! PUM! PUM! PUM! PUM! PUM! PUM! PUM! PUM! PUM! PUM!PUM! PUM!PUM!PUM!PUM!PUM!PUM! And thinner dotted lines of light zoomed up towards the silver crosses sailing calmly through the night.

A whistling. Thin, high-pitched, as if someone were expelling breath slowly through teeth and narrowed lips. The whistle sliding lower and lower in tone. The high whistling and the sliding down whistling all scrambled together. Crump!Crump!Crump!Crump! Crump!Crump! Crump! from far away. Crump!Crump!CruMP!CrUMP! CRUMP!CRUMP!! coming closer. The earth beginning to tremble, to vibrate.

The sounds all mixing. The whistling, high then sliding down. PUM!PUM!PUM!CRUMP!PUM!PUM!CRUMP! CRUMP!PUM!PUM!PUM!CRUMP!CRUMP!CRUMP! CRUMP!PUM!PUM!PUM!

The columns of light, the red flashes, the thin dotted lines of white. And, on the far side of the city, fiery blasts flaring up from the ground. The whistling sounds, the pounding of the explosions, the blue-white-red-white bursts all coming closer, closer.

Above, the little silver crosses gliding peacefully in the night. Except that, now and then, in less than a moment, one would disappear in a small puff of red light.

CRUMP!!!CRUMP!!!CRUMP!!!CRUMP!!!CRUMP!!!

The earth shuddering now, pulsating horribly under their feet, through their bodies. The screaming, the PUM!! PUM!!PUM!! no longer audible. Only CRUMP!!!! CRUMP!!!! CRUMP!!!!CRUMP!!!! of the explosions moving steadily through the city, right towards them.

Then they could hear nothing. The delicate membranes, the fragile bones of their ears could not transmit so much sound. But their eyes were filled with an incessant frenzy of dazzling light. And their bodies were linked to the thundering tempest that thudded upon the land. And passed over them.

And did not touch them.

Though the city burned. The fire at its centre towered into the sky, sucking in air from all around its base, feeding itself with whatever it found. The fire growing and growing. A storm of fire so fierce it turned all it touched into powdery ash, grey ash in low, sloping mounds. No streets, no houses, no buildings. Just smouldering mounds of colourless ash.

She wanted to wake up. Her head throbbed with pain. Her body ached. Perdue stood beside her. They held hands.

A new city rose from the ashes. Tall buildings lifted up, houses spread out, and moved closer, up to the rim of the garden.

Dawn came. The honey of sun poured over the city, the people up early to breathe the fresh air.

Then high, high up in a blue sky pellucid as crystal they saw, from their look-out on top of the house, a small glint of metal, heard a faint drone of sound. Saw it releasing a tiny black speck that blossomed two small white flowers and slowly floated down. The glinting metal, the drone of sound went away.

And there was *light*! The sun fallen to earth! The sun smashing down!

Light touched the people out in the streets. Their bodies puffed up, flesh cooking, falling off bones, bones seared to powder.

Light touched the buildings, blew them apart, burned them to ash.

The sun struck the earth, bursting back into sky. The sun exploded in a great sphere of purple and orange. At its core a pillar of flame, seething blood-dark, climbed up and far, far above billowed out, purple-white. A poisonous swelling of light.

Light touched the dome of the sky. Burned it black. The sky cracked in pieces. Black fragments of sky came tumbling down, smashed to the ground.

A flood filled the air, of charred pieces of sky, of all things touched by the light. It swept with a roar of oceans let loose, swirled round the garden.

Then silence.

The city was gone.

Above, where the sky used to be, were the stars. Now terribly bright, terribly near.

CHAPTER TWENTY

THEY WERE alive, unharmed by the exploding sun. Their faces were whole. The soft skin of cheeks, the delicate hair of eyebrows and lashes, the orbs of their eyes, the fragile satin of lips, all were entirely whole.

A gentle brushing of fingers touched faces. Trembling fingers touched lips and ears, tongue and teeth, hair, cheeks, the shape of noses, the shape of eyelids closed. Touched tears.

Touched as if they had never really understood such marvels before. Touched with hands the throb of pulse at throats, touched chests and breasts, touched nipples, touched the flat of bellies, the roundness of thighs. Touched the part that moistens to the touch, the part that rises to the touch. Touched with sliding hands, touched the back, the spine, the curving slopes of lower flesh.

Touched the body to the body. Touched. Lying down. Touched a firmness to a yielding. Touched the sliding in, the smooth enclosing. Touched and touched. Touched and touched. Touched the lips, the tongues, the mouths, the warm, the slow wet swirl of touch. Touched and touched. The sliding in of touch. The welcoming of touch. Touched and touched. Thunder surging. Touch of rain falling. Touched and touched. Touched and touched. Thunder. Wet touching. Touched and touched. Touched and touched. Touched and touched! Rain. Thunder! Rain touching. Touched and touched! Touched and touched! Touched and touched! Touched and touched! Lightning TOUCH! sizzling TOUCH! through the wet TOUCH! throbbing dark TOUCH! flowing through TOUCH! the copper roof TOUCH! into bodies TOUCH! frantic TOUCH! with the power TOUCH! flooding TOUCH! into them TOUCH! and dancing TOUCH! dancing! TOUCH! dancing! TOUCH! dancing! dancing! dancing! dancing!dancing!!dancing!!!

CHAPTER TWENTY-ONE

IT WAS NOT the pale light of dawn that woke her. It was the smell.

It should have been the smell of roses, the smell of prairie, the smell of the garden.

Perdue's arm was stretched over her belly, his head lay by her breasts. Her body was full of a wonderful ease and rest.

Above her, she saw the almost colourless new sky closing over the wounded heavens. Then, turning her head, she saw snow falling from almost invisible clouds. Beyond the rim of the warm, green garden, it already lay deep upon the land.

From the realm of the snow came the smell. A smell she knew. The smell of bodies rotting. Now close. And soon, she feared, to come closer.

All through the day, on the buffalo robes piled thick in her room, she and Perdue shared what their bodies could do with each other, while outside the snow continued to fall.

That night, astonished, exhausted, they slept.

In the strange, dim light of the next morning, they awoke to find snow arcing high above, seeming to float motionlessly over them upon an invisible dome. It was still warm inside this dome and the garden was untouched by frost, though only a faint trembling of sun could be seen at the very top.

Then the snow melted, swiftly unveiling a sky perfectly healed, perfectly blue.

And leaving behind great towers of glass, of silver and copper and steel, where the city had once stood. Towers that glittered like ice.

A fantastic new city of towers ablaze in the bright autumn day.

And machines, floating out of the sky, brought people to fill up the towers.

CHAPTER TWENTY-TWO

THEY HAD worked patiently, steadily. Starting from the edge of the inner circle of prairie, they brought the harvest home.

They pulled up great globes of onions, uprooted huge carrots and turnips, dug potatoes and picked tomatoes that they had to carry one at a time with both hands. They cut pumpkins, crookneck squash and acorn squash and vegetable marrow free from the enormous vines that had fed them, rolled them to the house, then rolled them carefully down a wooden chute into the cellar. They cut down the towering corn stalks with an axe, chopping the ears away from the stalk like branches from a tree. They scythed grain that stood higher than their outreaching arms, gathered it in sheaves, then into stooks. They flailed it, winnowed it. They cut flowers and herbs, carrying them inside.

The harvest filled the root cellar; it filled all the seed bins. It filled the empty rooms on the first floor. Soon vegetables lined the shelves of the library. Sacks and piles of vegetables covered the bare wooden floors. Mounds of dried beans and peas rested on each step in the spiral staircase.

The harvest filled the upstairs rooms, surrounding the pile of buffalo robes where they slept. It filled the attic. Herbs and flowers hung from the rafters, drying in the heat.

Where they had worked, the garden was layered with yellowing leaves and stalks and the tops of underground plants, with chaff from wheat and oats, from barley and rye. A golden carpet of plants calmly awaited return to the earth, the mixing and blending of what was left into the substance of a new season's life.

Now they lay on the Giant's stone, resting. Somehow the inner circle of prairie, the circle of roses, clung to the summer. The grass swayed supple and green in the wind, sprinkled with bright flowers. Rose blossoms covered the bushes, buds still swelling to flowers, the petals of full blooms finally dropping like tears, covering the stone.

While they had worked, they had not heard the tumult of sound from outside. Now it washed over them. They went into the house, climbed up the stairs to the attic, up to the look-out.

The towers of the city were connected by bustling streams of people moving from one tower to another. The hum of their voices drifted on the wind. But could only be heard as a murmuring tone that emerged now and then through the reverberating pronouncements of the machines.

Machines had laid networks of tracks across the land. Trains swooshed at incredible speeds along them. Massive machines rolled over the land itself, lifting away huge strips of soil, leaving behind what looked like white and grey rock. They loaded the soil onto trains. Other machines dug mine shafts into the earth, and soon to the surface came salt-white ore that was piled onto train after train.

To the south, as she looked through the binoculars, she saw a small train of shabby, old coaches stop at a mine-shaft. And a figure that seemed to be tall and incredibly strong got out. The giant figure helped something too bloated, too vast to be human, down from the train and into the mine. Then the machines underground returned to the surface and the mines were closed down, although she did not see the two figures emerge again.

Other trains came from the mountains. All the trains each had four or five engines and hundreds of open cars mounded with crushed rock of various shades, or with the blackness of coal. The mountains seemed to be sinking slowly into the earth.

Meanwhile, high open towers of metal had been raised all over the plain. Drills hung from their tops, and, rumbling and whining, dropped down to bore in the ground.

More trains came from the mountains.

The mountains subsided.

The sun slid down in the sky.

The last train pulled out.

The blue line of mountains was gone.

After supper, she and Perdue sat on the back steps, listening to the whine and throb of the drills as they bit through the earth. And so, when the machine floated down from the sky, landing right by the rim of the garden, and the dwarf stepped outside, they saw him at once. Saw him walk directly towards them. Saw how his suit of soft silver cloth, his shoes of bright silver, his helmet of silver, glittered and turned back the setting sun's light.

When he reached them, his hands and his face had a hard sheen of silver, did not look like skin. He spoke, his words coming out blurred, his jaw moving slowly, somehow unyielding to sound.

"We'll soon have it all." He tipped his head back at the closest drilling towers. "That's the last."

He looked at Perdue, then at her. His mouth moved slowly into a grimacing smile. "So I've come back for this."

His eyes, their silver centres gleaming, slid over her body. Lingered on her breasts, on the hair between her legs.

She felt a tight knot gather in her stomach. She clenched her hands. She would not go with him.

"Gold," he said, "silver . . . copper." He tried to laugh, the sound forcing itself out of his throat harshly. "The crops . . . then the soil. Potash . . . now oil." His mouth formed a sucking shape around the word "oil".

"Progress," he said. "Civilization." He pointed slowly to the sky. "New frontiers. Space."

With enormous roars, the towers blew apart, and in their place rose giant spouts of black liquid.

The dwarf turned as quickly as he could to look. He shouted, "Gushers!!"

The sun sank below a horizon bereft of mountains. In its last, long rays, the gushers gleamed like thick blood spurting out of the earth. It poured over the land, carrying with it a terrible stench. She remembered stories her mother and father had told her about the river of blood. The blood that seemed to have sunk underground, now welling forth, putrid and dark.

The dwarf tried to run, lurching strangely from side to side, towards the black blood. He thrashed through the cleared space of the garden, as the blood moved towards him. At the rim of the garden, they met, and he dipped down his hands and cupped up the thick, oozing fluid. He screamed in delight, trying to whirl around. The fluid lapped at his shoes, dripped down from his hands on to his suit. He shuffled forward into the fluid, dancing, laughing.

PERDUE
157

The dark liquid poured out faster, rose higher. It covered the land as far as the hills, covered the network of tracks, flowed all around the lustrous towers of the city. Quickly it mounted up to the knees of the dwarf, to his thighs. He turned, stumbling slowly back towards her and Perdue. Neither of them moved to help him. The black fluid rose to his waist, his chest. It was thicker than water, resisted all motion.

The dwarf opened his mouth to scream. The blood poured into his mouth, closed over his eyes, covered him all.

The sun disappeared.

Night, flowing out of the sky, flowing out of the earth, turned everything black, turned everything utterly still.

CHAPTER TWENTY-THREE

SHE LAY AWAKE. Perdue was asleep, his hand touching her side.

Against the window of their room, moths beat pale wings. The moon, now a tipped bowl spilling light, floated into her view.

She felt a movement in her belly, and slid her hands across its swelling shape. She looked down past her fuller breasts, her distended nipples, to the rounded skin. She felt the movement once again beneath her fingers, the life stirring there.

She thought her touch could sense, below her own strong, beating heart, a fainter echo of that beat.

Perdue turned, closed eyes facing the moon. The scar where the dwarf had wounded him gleamed whitely. He turned back to her, nestling his head near her breast. She held him close with her arm.

She felt at peace, calm, but also had a sense that things were moving to completion, that soon all this would change.

The moon passed by the window.

Her eyelids fluttered like the wings of moths, closed.

She fell asleep.

CHAPTER TWENTY-FOUR

THE GIANT'S stone was still as warm as if the midsummer sun had been soaking into it all day. But the roses around it, struck by a killing frost, hung their leaves limp and brown. Most of the blossoms, shrivelled, blackened, had fallen. The flowers of the prairie, too, had been killed. And the long grasses bent in a withered tangle that no longer swayed to the ripple of the freezing wind.

Crouching on the stone, they saw a flotilla of vast, hovering shapes trail thin, shining snouts to suck up the sea of oil that covered the land. When they had it all, they floated away, heading south towards the lowered, winter sun.

Other floating machines landed on the pinnacles of the towers. They filled up with all of the people, and followed the other fleet. The empty towers stood silent, icy and still.

The smell of decay had grown stronger, even though the oil was gone. It clutched at their throats, trying to choke them.

CHAPTER TWENTY-FIVE

THE PARCHED CLAY of the earth, its soil stripped entirely away, was stained black. It felt cold and hard beneath their feet. The air was chill, the wind rising. Yet they walked on. The moon, pushing to fullness, glided through the pale sky, moving closer to the declining sun.

They reached the towers, which rose so high, throwing back from the dazzling heights all of the remaining light. They walked through the dark-stained streets that were totally empty, the people all gone. Leaving the ghostly towers to crumble and fall at the end of their time.

The sun and the moon touched. The sky dimmed. The moon and the sun slid together. Light went out of the sky, drained away from the luminous towers. In the swift dark, they took on the darkness of the stained earth at their base. Instead of seeming to soar into space, they loomed as if about to topple, threatening.

The moon covered the sun. Around it, a corona of light flickered. The moon wore a crown of light.

A freezing wind came wailing over the land from somewhere far. Brought with it the powerful stench of decay. The decay of something still living, but only kept alive by living on death. Brought with it a tremor of sound, a terrible cry composed from the moments life goes out of things. The smell and the cry of things ending.

She knew what this was. Saw that somehow Perdue knew it too.

This thing wanting blood. This thing that knew she was a true child of blood. That a child grew inside her.

This was the smell, this was the cry of He-Who-Lives-Alone.

She remembered the stories she had heard, huddling in a cave of earth in the winter's cold, sheltering under fur. When blizzards moaned for days, and hunger gnawed, her parents warned her of the Windigo.

The wind whistled stronger. The air, suddenly colder, cut to the bone. Away to the north, they saw a towering shape hidden by swirling snow. The snow a disguise to hide the true, horrible form of the creature inside.

She grasped Perdue's hand.

Quickly, they turned back to the shelter of their home.

PART

3

CHAPTER ONE

THE SUN and the moon had fallen out of the sky.

She and Perdue could not see each other's faces. The sound of gasping breath filled the dark room. Their hands rested on the smooth, large roundness of her belly, within which something moved and struggled. She gasped hard, sharp breaths. Her body throbbed, the muscles of the belly squeezing. She propped herself up against the wall, raised her knees, spread her legs.

And then appeared a faint glimmer of light. There, between her thighs. Something emerging. A small, rounded bulge pushing out. A surface that glistened, that pulsed with a pale glow. Her body shuddered rhythmically. She gasped, gasped. The small round surface pushed further out. She shuddered.

Perdue found himself looking at a glowing forehead, at

tiny, closed eyes. The whole face emerged: the neck, the shoulders twisted sideways. Her body shuddered. Miniature hands, clenched shut, were crossed and rested on the chest. The child opened its mouth as if to cry out in greeting, but did not.

By the pale light that came forth from the child, they saw the shapes of their own bodies emerge from the darkness. Perdue slid a finger under each of the child's arms, helping the small body to glide all the way out of its mother. He lifted the child gently onto her belly, settling it front down, its arms and its legs folded under, its face turned to one side. She felt its weight. It was warm as summer.

The child, covered with a thick, white coating, lay there quietly. From the centre of its belly, a twisting cord of flesh connected it still to the inside of her. The cord throbbed with blood. The child took one breath, stopped.

She put out her hands to touch the child. It floated upon the warm rise and fall of her soft skin. The child yawned and stretched, began to welcome this new substance—air —more and more into its body, began to uncurl itself, reaching out to discover space, unenclosed space. The cord stopped beating. Powerful waves surged from one end of the child's body to the other. She felt something attached to the end of the cord, glistening blue and red, slide out of her.

Now the child was completely separate from her body. And it glowed. Glowed with a light that flickered and waned, then grew stronger again. The bright shape of the child glowed in her eyes and the eyes of Perdue, and they saw that shape there when they looked at each other.

The shining child drove away the darkness of the room.

CHAPTER TWO

THE SHRIEKING wind circled the house.

They woke up shivering. In their sleep, they had pulled a buffalo robe over themselves and the child. Nonetheless they were cold, although the sleeping child was perfectly warm.

Then they heard the house, creaking and groaning. A harsh, thin illumination pushed through the windows. And a vicious wind seemed, as they watched, to force the glass from its frame, sending it flying into the room to shatter upon the floor. Then the freezing wind swirled in, carrying with it a dreadful stench and an eerie moaning.

At once, they gathered up the child, grabbed one of the robes. They knew they must try to escape, to save the child. They stumbled across the room, slashed by the gusting cold. The stench swept into their lungs.

GEOFFREY URSELL
168

The house trembled, shook. Paint fell in huge flakes from the ceiling. The wallpaper faded, grew enormous stains, and peeled off in tattered strips and shreds. Beneath their feet, the floor boards shifted, the golden wood discolouring. Squealing nails shot free. The floor buckled, sending them lurching towards the door to the hall. From the attic above and the rooms around, they could hear the crash of falling plaster. They reached the hall.

Behind them, the bedroom ceiling caved in with a roar. The house shuddered, screamed. They staggered down the hall, clutching the warm child and the buffalo robe.

In the rooms and hallways where the harvest had rested, vegetables rotted into pulp and mounds of seeds withered into dust before their eyes. Glass exploded on the shaking floor. The icy wind shrieked triumphantly throughout the house.

They stumbled down the stairs. As soon as their feet had left it, the spiral staircase collapsed thunderously into the cellar, leaving a jagged, gaping hole in the floor. They reached the front door, which hung half-open from one rusted hinge. They put their shoulders to it, nearly falling as it exploded into splinters at their touch. All at once they were out in the bitter chill, the stench, the screaming wind.

As they turned back to look at it, the house shook from side to side, tottering on its foundation. Mortar, expelled from between the heavy stones of the walls, fell all around. In a final convulsion, the walls plunged in upon one another, the roof beams plummeting down upon the rubble with a resounding shock as wood and metal met rock.

A terrible stench surrounded them. A dreadful cry beat upon their ears. Coming towards them they saw a dark cloud, a whirlwind of snow.

They leaned into the wind, trying to reach the Giant's stone. The wild prairie grass and the rose bushes around it, tossed by the frenzy of the wind, crumbled to dust. They ran over naked earth that had suddenly become as hard and bare as frozen rock.

They reached the stone.

The whirlwind came closer, the awful odour and sound increasing, the wintry cold intensifying.

They stepped upon the stone and turned to face the whirlwind. The child was warm in their arms, the stone warm as summer beneath their feet.

For an instant, they thought they saw an immense twisted figure, looming up over them.

Then the stone fell, plunging them into the earth.

CHAPTER THREE

THEY DROPPED into the depths of the earth. Looking up, they saw a small circle of white shrink and dwindle into a pin-point, then vanish.

They fell, holding each other close, falling until it seemed they were motionless. And then it seemed as if they were falling back through time, through eons of existence they knew nothing about, except that there had been other lives, there had been living things filling the world long before them. Things that were buried in this blur of earth and stone into which they were sinking.

The stone seemed to have reached its highest speed. They fell and fell, without seeming to fall, suspended in the dark, until the motion became familiar, not fearful at all. Their bodies relaxed, falling down, down, down.

And at the same moment that it occurred to them that they must come to a stop somewhere, and they must—at such a speed—all be killed when they hit bottom, at that moment the stone began to slow its descent, to lessen the speed of its fall. Soon it slowed even more, until, with a gentle thud, it stopped.

They had followed the trace the Giant's body had made nearly two centuries before as it had plunged through the earth, the same kind of trace a meteorite makes as it burns through the air. Now they were deep in the dark. Between them, the glow of the uncovered child flickered. By that light, they saw that they were not enclosed. There was an empty space around them.

They stepped off the stone.

A vivid flower of light bloomed in the darkness, revealing to them the dimensions of a tunnel wide and high enough to accommodate the destroyed house. The tunnel opened out in both directions. It went on and on, a column of light narrowing to a point. And yet—they could sense—went far beyond what they could see.

The walls of the tunnel were white tinged with pink, and gleamed and glittered in the light. She and Perdue looked at the walls more closely. They were a mass of milky crystals, here and there quite pure, but mostly washed through with the pale red of wild roses.

It must be, they thought, that some of the blood of the slaughtered buffalo, the blood of the slaughtered people, had seeped down through the earth, seeped down to colour these walls.

They each wet a finger on their tongues and touched it to the crystals. They licked the powder that clung there.

Their mouths filled with the taste of tears.

GEOFFREY URSELL
172

CHAPTER FOUR

THEY STOOD at the centre of an enormous cross of light. Before and behind, and on either side, intersecting tunnels stretched luminously into the distance. The air was hot, humid.

They had wandered into a vast maze of tunnels and now no longer knew where they were. Whenever they reached a place where the tunnels crossed, the new tunnel would light up. And, if they turned to follow it, the tunnel they had left would grow dark behind them. So they walked on, always in light, leaving darkness behind, walking towards darkness.

They hoped to find a place where the grid stopped, or its centre. But the tunnels were all the same, all empty, all silent. White crystal walls stained pale red glinting in the brilliant, harsh light.

They turned to the left. The tunnel they had abandoned grew dark. They walked on. The warm child slept, always slept, cradled in their arms. Their bare feet moved easily upon the powdery dust of the floor.

All they could do was walk, sharing the burden of the child. They stopped briefly when the child wanted to suckle, stretching out on the buffalo robe and rubbing the soreness out of their legs.

And, in the stillness, they thought they could hear a faint murmur, a deep pulse of something moving slowly, surging even deeper in the earth.

There was no water in the tunnels: only the crystals tasting of tears, only the dried remains of the blood. Their mouths and tongues grew dry. To wet them, Perdue sucked a small amount of the warm milk from her breasts. Not swallowing, he placed his mouth on hers, and they shared the sweet fluid.

They passed entrances of tunnel after tunnel, an enormous labyrinth the machines had carved out in their quest for the buried potash, the treasure of fertilizer, hidden under the prairie. The intersecting tunnels turned light as they reached them, darkened as they walked on. Glancing along these tunnels, they saw that all were the same— long, luminescent passages that seemed to go on forever. As did the tunnel they walked in.

They wondered if, far above them, it were night or day. Here they moved in a perpetual false and glaring light that streamed forth from the apex of the tunnels. They could not get away from the light.

Walking on and on, they had the sensation that they were not walking, that they were standing in one place. And that, by the pressure of their feet, they were pulling the tunnel towards them and pushing it behind them. That they were caught in a huge circling tunnel in which they passed by the same points again and again.

GEOFFREY URSELL
174

The child slept, never making a sound. They walked on. Through the light. Through the silence. Only the whisper of naked feet treading dust.

At last, exhausted and hungry, they threw down the buffalo robe, lay on it, and joined the child in sleep.

CHAPTER FIVE

THE SOUND rose up from the earth beneath them, echoing deep and hollow, rhythmic and endless. When they opened their eyes, pale blue-green light flooded in, a milky blue-green that thickened to emerald when they looked down, to milky green when they looked up. They were suspended in light, their limbs moving slowly, drifting out from their bodies. Far above, long, thin shafts of light hung, hovering and shifting. The hollow throb of the sound went on and on, beating steadily in their bodies.

The child joined them together, one of their hands each enclosing one of its tiny hands. Its eyes were still closed. They felt peaceful, yet filled with a growing happiness.

With languid motions, they turned to look into the depths. Far below, the undulating foliage of plants they had never seen before nearly hid the dappled rock and sand. The long dark-green leaves, the leaves the texture and colour of old lace, creamy-brown, the leaves like soft yellow fingers, all waved in a fluid wind. Here and there amidst the plants, red or blue tubes pulsated, among small mounds of purple or green, spiky with black points. Another tube shape held a mass of tapering pale-green fronds that gently explored the surrounding space.

They looked more closely at things gliding amidst the plants, at things scuttling across the rock and sand. Things with claws and eyes on the top of quivering stalks crawled about. Things the form of stars, orange or azure-blue, pulled themselves along. Things dwelling inside shells moved placidly. There were countless kinds of shells: round and fluted shells, shells wrapped in circles or spiral-ling into cones, shells ridged and smooth. And the shells had bands of delicate pale tints or bright dots and flecks of rainbow hues.

They turned again, drifting up through this astonish-ing, vital world. A great triangular creature, dark-brown on top and white underneath, sailed by with swaying wings, almost touching them. Multitudes of smaller crea-tures, iridescent with stripes and splotches of colour, darted this way and that in unison, as if they were one, not a thousand separate beings. A thing with a fluent, mottled-green body surged by, its eight long arms turning their pale-brown suckers to fondle their limbs as it passed. And large beasts with rough hides, their mouths gaping with rows of needled teeth, stared at them with blank eyes.

But they felt no danger, only a gathering joy, as they moved away from the beasts, rising towards the milky green above. Gliding by a colossal mottled-blue mass that turned an enormous eye curiously towards them, they were greeted by several sleek creatures with pale-blue bellies and glistening black backs, who nuzzled their pale bodies and mouthed their fingers softly. As they rose, they saw that they must pass through shimmering clouds of innumerable tiny things, clouds of green, clouds of orange, before they joined the creatures frolicking beyond, disappearing and reappearing over their heads. Creatures their size, with large, lustrous eyes and long whiskers. Creatures larger, with wrinkled brown skin, and long pointed teeth emerging from their mouths.

And now they rose, exalted, into the wavering beams of light, gliding faster and faster, in company with the sleek beings who pirouetted round and round them, their glistening bodies flashing, vibrant with energy. The child rising faster than they, lifting above their heads, seeming to pull them faster and faster up to the light. The throb of the surging sound pounding through them. The milky-green becoming clear, translucent. The light brighter and brighter.

The child burst through, pulling them too, and they all burst out of the sea and soared into the sun and the spume of waves in the wind, soared into the sky, the creatures with them leaping high, all in a glory of air and light.

GEOFFREY URSELL

CHAPTER SIX

THEY AWOKE from their dream to a sound.

The faintest of hums.

In their ears and not there. And again in their ears. They tilted their heads, straining to listen, to discover the source of the sound. And could not.

They got up and walked. Stopped. Listened again. The hum was no longer there. They retraced their steps. Again, the hum.

They walked on. Twisting through the labyrinth of tunnels, following the sound. Gradually it grew from the hum they had first heard into a buzz, then into a rumbling whine. Louder and louder.

Soon the sound was as much a part of the tunnels as the glare of light. Then it became overwhelming, an incessant thundering roar that trembled through the floor of the tunnel into their bodies. When they paused, the vibrations surged through them. The child slept on, oblivious.

She and Perdue looked at each other, wondering if they should go on. It seemed that the tunnels would be shaken into collapse by the force of the vibrations. They turned to look back down the tunnel. In the far distance, a haze filled the air. They moved towards it.

The reverberation grew even louder, numbing their ears. The haze enveloped them, thickening into a powdery mist. They took in sipping breaths, yet the powder invaded their nostrils, their mouths, their lungs with the smell, with the taste of tears. The powder sifted down, covering their bodies with a milky film. They held hands, moving carefully forward, their eyes blinking away the powder to let them see.

The tunnel convulsed with shudders, with pealing incessant thunder, with seething dust.

Suddenly, silence.

And out of the thick haze before them, the billowing cloud of ancient deaths, a shape took form. A shape she had seen going into the mine. A shape familiar to Perdue, although he had never imagined he would see it again.

The shape of the Giant.

CHAPTER SEVEN

THEY SAT on the edges of the buffalo robe, with the sleeping child in the centre. The Giant had taken off the mask that made his face a featureless sphere, and Perdue now saw that this was not the Giant he had known. This Giant had a lighter skin, had a golden mustache and beard, had long, golden hair that fell in curls around his shoulders. Yet, like the other Giant, his body too radiated a warmth like that of a summer day.

The Giant opened up a large flask and handed it to them. The water inside was ice-cold, and she and Perdue gulped down the wonderful, chill liquid.

The Giant had turned off the machine, one of those designed to mine the potash. It stood quiet now, a mass of glinting silver metal that covered the entire end of the tunnel. The white powder that rested in a thick layer all over the Giant's body was settling out of the air on all of them. They could breathe more easily, and they could see without constantly blinking their eyes.

The child lay, breathing peacefully in its perpetual sleep, between them. The Giant carefully watched how its body glimmered with a warm, flickering glow.

When he had finished drinking, Perdue undid the thong that held the pouch at his side. He placed the pouch on the robe in front of him and loosened its fastening. The Giant looked from the child to Perdue. Perdue handed the Giant the pouch. As soon as the Giant took it, the finger bones inside began to clatter. The Giant held the pouch straight out in front of him, and tipped it open.

The finger bones of the Giant who had been Perdue's friend tumbled out. They drifted slowly down, turning over and over. Even as they fell, they began to take the shape of a circle. The circle of bones fell around the child, enclosing it.

They all looked at the circle of bones, at each other.

They reached out, joining hands in yet another circle around the child.

GEOFFREY URSELL
182

CHAPTER EIGHT

THE GIANT removed a huge silver cube from the machine. Perdue saw that it was exactly the same size and shape as the keystone, the gravestone. The Giant spread their robe out on its top and lifted them up to sit on it. Then, without any apparent effort, he put his arms along the side of the cube, pushed his fingers underneath it, and hoisted it straight up in front of him. And, with his eyes peering out over the top and looking between their bodies, he began to run.

The dark tunnels to either side flashed briefly with light, then darkened at once as they rushed past. Their long hair flowed out straight behind them, floating in the rush of air. The Giant's feet seemed hardly to touch the floor in his flight. The walls of the tunnels blurred, as they hurtled by.

The Giant ran on and on, yet his breathing was easy and

slow, no deeper than when he had sat beside them. And his forehead was absolutely dry, did not have a drop of moisture on it. He ran faster than any buffalo, faster than Sir's stallion. He ran smoothly. His body was warm with a summery warmth, but he did not sweat.

They twisted and turned through the labyrinth of tunnels, at last reaching the dark shape of a tunnel opening only on their left. They entered the new tunnel. No lights came on. The dimensions of this new space slid away into the dark. The Giant stopped.

All at once, a great pillar of light blazed up from the floor, soared straight up into the darkness, striking the roof of the cavern high, high overhead. They saw that they were in an immense dome carved out of the crystal, which here was stained a deeper red, a dark crimson. Beneath the Giant's feet, the powdery floor was the bright scarlet colour of blood.

Down from the top of the pillar of light floated a silver platform. It fell slowly, poised in the centre of the light. It stopped, hovering well above the cavern floor.

Standing at its centre was a man. A naked man. A monstrously fat man. The bloated shape she had also seen enter the mine with the Giant.

The man's arms stuck out almost straight from his sides. They could not be lowered because of the corpulent bulk of his chest. His huge belly descended in ever-larger folds down nearly to his knees. His genitals were completely hidden beneath the mass of hanging flesh. He balanced upon legs like the stumps of two massive trees.

The man was also incredibly old. His skin was a complex network of criss-crossing wrinkles, puffy and yet deeply creased, like the skin of mouldering potatoes. Upon this grotesque body perched a diminutive head, from which long straggles of yellow-white hair dangled. A blood-red crown encircled the head, held up by a bull neck.

Perdue looked closely. He knew this man. It was the

man who had taken away Gal Sal. It was His Highness Most Serene.

His Highness spoke.

"I don't know why you've come," he said, his voice a harsh cawing, a croaking. "There's nothing for you here."

In the pouch at Perdue's side, the finger bones clattered together, then were silent.

His Highness glanced at the sleeping child and at her, then looked directly at Perdue.

"There's nothing for you here," he repeated. He turned his gaze upon the Giant. "Now," he said, his voice cajoling, yet filled with threat, "give me what you have."

The Giant put the silver cube down and helped them off. He slid the top of the cube open, then lifted it up as easily as if it were a bale of hay. He carried the open cube over to the platform and with one swift motion tipped it over.

Out of the silver metal billowed a cloud of darkest crimson. His Highness Most Serene reached out his open hands towards it. It pulsated wildly as it flowed into the brilliant light. Instantly, the cloud soared in the dazzling column. His Highness disappeared, although they could still hear his voice.

"*Blood!*" he said in a quavering scream. "Blood! Blood! Blood!"

The crimson cloud transformed the shaft of light into a vibrant artery of luminous red. The blood surged up, a pillar of deep scarlet, the palpitating centre of the dark cavern.

"Go-o-ood!" they heard. "*Go-o-o-oood!!*"

The platform rose, and the shaft of brilliant blood vanished, leaving them once more in darkness.

Within moments, the platform and the pillar of light had returned, carrying upon it a brimming container of chill water and a large oblong chunk of something the colour of cream.

These the Giant lifted off the platform. He tipped the container and began pouring it into his mouth. He shoved the block of food to his lips and began biting off large chunks, chewing and swallowing rapidly.

The column of light flickered out. In the pitch-black, the body of the child who did not wake was once more visible, radiating a wavering glow. The Giant loomed up above the child, the pale shape of the infant reflected in his eyes.

The child stirred in its sleep, moving its mouth in a sucking motion. She picked up the child and put it to her breast. The child, its eyes still closed, took the nipple in its mouth and fed.

The Giant, looking at the small body of the child, held out the water and the food to her, to Perdue.

GEOFFREY URSELL

CHAPTER NINE

THE FINGER bones rattled in their pouch, warning them of the descent of His Highness upon his platform even before the pillar of light sprang up. He hovered over them. His body was thick with blood-red powder, its dark crimson lining all the creases and seams in his ancient flesh. His bulging lips drooled red froth. His voice slurred, crawling over his words.

"My son," he said. "My son."

The blood powder dribbled from his clenched fists.

The Giant stood facing the blob of red body. His eyes looked up directly into the bloodshot orbs of His Highness Most Serene.

"You have done well, my son," His Highness said. "Except—" his voice slid through the hot, still air, vicious and sibilant. "Except, what I gave you was for no one else."

Beads of blood dripped from his skin, as if it were rotting with primeval decay. His eyes narrowed, glared. His mouth twisted into a wet, red slit.

"Do you so quickly forget what you owe me?" he demanded. "You, who are guilty of so much. Look!"

He threw out his hand, and, in the column of light below His Highness, a scene with two figures appeared. Upon a bed lay a woman, her belly an enormous mound pinning her down. It was Gal Sal. Her arms and legs, spread out, were rigid with pain. Her body dripped with sweat. She moaned and wept.

"You are guilty," His Highness insisted. "Guilty!"

Beside Gal Sal stood the dwarf, in black cape and cream-white suit. He lifted his cane, took out the sword inside. Gal Sal moaned, she beat her arms upon the bed.

"You would not be born. You had to be born!"

The dwarf, with a quick slash of the blade, cut open Gal Sal's belly, far deeper than he had cut Perdue. Gal Sal screamed, a high, piercing wail. The dwarf thrust his hands into the wound, pulling the flesh back from the body of a giant child inside.

"You killed your mother! You killed her, my son!"

The dwarf struggled to pull the child free. Gal Sal kept screaming. The giant child was almost as large as the dwarf. The child emerged, coated with blood and a slippery white film. Gal Sal stopped screaming. Her body went limp.

The dwarf's suit dripped with blood.

The scene disappeared.

The finger bones rattled in their pouch.

"You must be punished," His Highness wheezed, sucking air into his buried lungs, the effort of breathing opening his mouth wide.

"You will get nothing more until they are dead. You will hunger and thirst, until you try to eat these very walls. You will fill your mouths with blood and salt, and scream out for my help, for my forgiveness." He began to laugh. "Eating blood." The laughing mouth opened wide, drooling red froth. "Eating salt!"

They thought they heard something more than the laughter reverberating through the cavern. Something rhythmic and endless, surging, a muted sound rolling deep and resonant. The sound from their dream.

The bones lurched fiercely, pulling the pouch tight on the thong that held it at Perdue's side. The Giant turned to look. Perdue undid the thong, and once more handed the pouch to the Giant.

"You will come crawling to me, my son!" His Highness said to the Giant, then laughed and laughed.

The bones clacked angrily together. The Giant began to undo the thong that held captive the finger bones of his true father. All the while he watched His Highness coldly.

The thong loosened and the bones leapt free, soaring through the air, forming hands that flew at the swollen, burbling throat of His Highness. He did not see them coming, did not have time to blink. The bony hands had his bull-like throat in their strangling grasp.

His Highness tried to shriek, but no sound emerged. His mouth widened into a dark pit. He tried to claw at the bones, but his arms would not bend, his own hands could not reach his throat.

They watched the life going out of His Highness Most Serene. His face turned purplish-black, his body sagged at the knees, dropping to its side on the platform.

Their power finally gone, the bones fell away.

The Giant went to the platform. Carefully, he gathered the bones together, tenderly placing them inside the pouch, and fastened it around his neck.

PERDUE

189

CHAPTER TEN

THEY HAD not noticed the wind.

It whistled through the tunnels and into the cavern, harsh and powerful. It swirled the crimson particles of the floor into the air, stinging their bodies. Then the icy chill brought by the wind touched them, and they all smelled the stench of something long dead but still somehow living, and they all heard the terrible cry of things ending.

The wind spun round and round. The smell and the sound of death grew stronger, almost overpowering. Their shivering bodies felt numbed, the heat of life being stolen from them. They gathered up the child, still somehow warm with a summery warmth, and held it close.

Then the whirlwind slowed and finally fell away. And before them stood the figure of the Windigo, He-Who-Lives-Alone.

He-Who-Lives-Alone was taller than the Giant. His head was enormous, his face black with frost-bite. Peeling flesh hung down from his cheeks. His lips had been completely eaten away by cold, disclosing the long fangs of his teeth. His breath came out in clouds of ice crystals, hissing and whistling through his teeth. He opened his mouth wide and out came a roar that reverberated around the cavern. His eyes protruded, rolling in blood that dripped from their corners, freezing upon his frost-stripped face.

Yet all his features were blurred, as if he were moving too fast for their eyes to follow, or as if he were shifting in and out of his shape continually.

He-Who-Lives-Alone swung his gaze over the room, resting it at last upon the body of His Highness Most Serene. On feet with long pointed heels and only one great toe on each foot, feet that seemed to be aflame when they moved, he leapt at the corpse. He grabbed the body with his hands, the long claw-like fingers and nails ripping into the dead flesh. With one swift motion, he tore the body in half and lifted the halves high, tipping back his head and opening his twisted mouth wide to catch the blood that poured from it.

They could see the still-hot blood flowing into the frozen cage of bones that was his chest, bathing in warmth the shape of ice that was his heart.

He sucked the last drops of blood from the body as it froze solid in his grasp. Finished, he flung the halves of the body against the wall of the cavern, where it shattered, like ice, into countless fragments.

Then he turned to face them again. He howled, a long-drawn-out, thunderous howl. That horrible sound, composed of the moments life goes out of things, stunned and appalled them. His putrid breath swirled around them. He-Who-Lives-Alone raised his arms wide, stretching out his claw-like fingers.

She and Perdue held each other close, sheltering the child who did not wake.

He-Who-Lives-Alone lunged for them.

But the Giant stepped between.

PERDUE

191

CHAPTER ELEVEN

THE SHOCK of their first meeting shook the cavern. Beneath her feet, and Perdue's, the earth rocked.

He-Who-Lives-Alone, repulsed, screamed in unbelieving rage and frustration at this check. Then they heard the Giant's voice too, an answering sound that met that deathly scream, a sound as strong, but gentle.

Then the towering figures met again, moving so quickly that she and Perdue could hardly see the frightful battle, the blur of dreadful combat surging all around the cavern.

Yet from that struggle rose an aromatic exhalation to counteract the stench, a marvellous odour, the incredible smell, Perdue suddenly remembered, made by the first Giant and Gal Sal. This smell had wafted over the land, and, in their cave below the crest of the river valley, the lonely couple and their small child had smelled it too, this mysterious trace of the vanished wild and unbroken prairie. She, once that child, remembered this smell as well as did Perdue. And in their arms their child stirred, seeming to respond to its summons.

And all at once they knew that the sound the Giant made was a sound composed of spring and summer winds, a sound of things being born, a sound of new and thriving life. The smell and sound of life's profusion, of life's splendour.

And again they heard, rolling below the pitch of battle, something more, a surging force below them, waiting to be free.

As the Giant and He-Who-Lives-Alone fought, that sonorous thunder grew, until the whole cavern shook not only with their encounter, but with the pulse of a great hidden power.

They saw He-Who-Lives-Alone grasp the Giant in his arms, striving to crush out his life. And then the Giant bursting clear, pulling He-Who-Lives-Alone off his feet, whirling him around and around over his head and smashing him into the earth so that the earth split. And that incredible force held back by the earth broke loose, a geyser exploding, hurling the screaming He-Who-Lives-Alone high to the dome and holding him there, dissolving his rib cage of ice and finding its way to his frozen heart and melting him all the way into nothing.

And the Giant gathered them up in his arms, away from the sea of water surging up from the cavern's core, lifting them safe from the maelstrom of sea and running as swift as could be, the sea booming behind them down the tunnels, filling them up in an instant. The Giant running and reaching the stone that had brought them into this underground world, setting them down on the stone and lifting it up over his head, as the Giant now dead had once lifted Perdue, lifting them up through the roof of the tunnel, the sea surging towards him even as they rose above his head, swallowing him up, but they, above him, lifted. The Giant gone, and the sea let loose now lifting them up, up, up at incredible speed, pushing them up like a cork through a tube, until at the top they exploded, the stone flung high in the air and far, reaching a height and then falling, falling again to the earth of the highest ridge of hills. The stone dropping down, and she and Perdue transfixed and unmoving, holding the child, borne on the stone, the stone falling to earth.

And they found themselves standing, feet on the level of the land on the ridge. And Perdue remembered how the cavalcade, with his father in the lead on a stallion, finally came out of the forest and reached this very spot, and looked out upon the vast expanse of plain.

And the sea burst free, washing the earth in the tears of weeping generations, cleansing it with tears, baptizing it with tears.

And she and Perdue wept, for the Giant now lost, tears flowing down their faces, their cheeks wet, tears anointing their eyes, and their eyes open upon the darkness of the night, no moon, the stars far, far points of fire. And the sleeping child stirred, the glowing child awakened, the child lifted its head and opened its eyes. And its eyes were sparkling orbs of radiant light!

GEOFFREY URSELL

CHAPTER TWELVE

INTO THE VAULT of black above the northern horizon, an arc of ethereal light rose up. Its great luminous curve lifted higher and higher, its fiery base issuing flames of pale, translucent green. The ends of the arc pulled free of the earth, and the streamers of light rippled and fluttered, releasing new ribbons of flame that fluently echoed the shimmering brilliance, the fast-shifting flow.

The child, awake, its eyes ablaze, welcomed into its life the dance of the spirits of all who had died. The flickering glow of the child's body grew, pulsing stronger and stronger.

From the dance in the sky they heard faint swishing cries, the songs of the spirits. And from the child's throat came an answering cry, a sound forming into a new song of enchantment.

The flow of the light moved faster, mounting into the dark; flared yellow and bluish-white; fragmented into flashing shafts, into swirling sheets of fire. The stars vanished behind the splendour that leapt overhead, climbing the night sky to the zenith. And there the light converged, the resplendent light, a corona, a crown.

The child, responding, its eyes now dazzlingly bright, its body transparent with light, throbbed with such force that she and Perdue could not watch any more. Though the song of the child, joined with the songs of the northern night dancers, poured into their ears, filling them up with rapture.

And they turned their gaze out to see where the celestial light shone on the sea that flooded the land, its sparkling reflection thrown back by the ocean of tears pouring out of the earth and dissolving the towers that fell silently down, disappeared.

GEOFFREY URSELL

CHAPTER THIRTEEN

IT WAS NOT the pale light of dawn that woke them.

It was the smell.

It should have been the smell of sea, the tang of salt spray from the rolling billows breaking in spumes of foam upon the shores of what had been the hills. The smell of a vast ocean reaching out to the circle of sky, light glinting off its blue-green depths. The smell of tears.

They stood up, holding the child between them. The sun had just risen behind their backs, and from the top of the ridge of hills their shadows should have stretched out enormously long, spindly and dark. But they held the child, and the child was ablaze with light.

So they cast no shadow upon the land.

The land! A vast expanse of plain rolling out and away to the purple blur of the horizon. And the warm summer wind flowing over the land filled up their nostrils with a strange, keen fragrance, compounded of wild grasses swaying in the breeze, of wild flowers surging up to the spring sun, prairie roses bursting open, of blossoms on chokecherry, buffalo berry, and saskatoon bushes, the leaves of wolf willow.

The pungent whirlwind of scent, the marvellous smell of wild, unbroken prairie.

GEOFFREY URSELL